The Whipsaw Trail

RAY HOGAN

The Whipsaw Trail

A DOUBLE D WESTERN
DOUBLEDAY
New York   London   Toronto   Sydney   Auckland

A Double D Western
PUBLISHED BY DOUBLEDAY
a division of Bantam Doubleday Dell Publishing Group, Inc.
666 Fifth Avenue, New York, New York 10103

A Double D Western, Doubleday,
and the portrayal of the letters DD
are trademarks of Doubleday, a division of
Bantam Doubleday Dell Publishing Group, Inc.

Library of Congress Cataloging-in-Publication Data

Hogan, Ray, 1908–
    The whipsaw trail / Ray Hogan. — 1st ed.
        p.   cm. — (A Doubleday D western)
    I. Title.
    PS3558.O3473W48   1992
    813'.54—dc20   91-20670
    CIP

ISBN 0-385-41595-8
Copyright © 1992 by Ray Hogan
All Rights Reserved
Printed in the United States of America
January 1992
First Edition

W

10   9   8   7   6   5   4   3   2   1

for . . .
Gwynn, Scott, Mike, and Darlene

The Whipsaw Trail

ONE

JOHN BUCKNER tossed aside the butt of the stogie he had been smoking and glanced about. A tight grin parted his lips. He was mighty calm for a man about to rob a bank, he thought, one that was not only in the center of a town, but in broad daylight as well. On the other hand he reckoned it maybe was not so unusual after all; when it came right down to hardrock, he really wasn't holding up the bank, he was just collecting money owed him for five years or so. Moreover, it wouldn't be the bank's money he'd be taking, it would be money that belonged to the railroad.

Keeping back in the shadows lying alongside the low, flat-roofed building, he studied Grovertown's main street. It was quiet at this not yet midmorning hour with only a few people abroad going about their various chores. A wagon was pulled up in front of Horn's General Store, and Jim McKinley, who operated the stageline depot, was making ready for the west-bound coach due to arrive in about a half hour. Off to the west crows were cawing as they flapped their way to the fields below town.

John brushed at the sweat beading his forehead. It was not from nervousness but from the warmth of the day. In truth he was as cool as he would be were he ordering a meal at the settlement's favorite restaurant. He knew exactly what he would do in the minutes that lay ahead. He had spent the better part of the month in the South Missouri town working out his plan and detailing it down to the last moment.

He knew when the bank would most likely be deserted insofar as customers were concerned, and that there would be only C. W. Pruitt, the firm's owner, and his clerk on hand. Also he had chosen the end of the month, May in this case, when fares collected by the several rail and stage-line points along the line had been turned in to be forwarded to the home office in St. Louis. If his observations were right there would be more money in the shipment satchel than the five thousand dollars he intended to take.

He planned to ride west once he had his money, angling across southwest Missouri into Indian Territory, on to Texas and into New Mexico. From there circumstance would dictate his route to Mexico; he would either head due south along the Rio Grande to the border, or cut over into the somewhat new territory of Arizona, once the western half of New Mexico but created a separate area by Confederate General John Baylor around the beginning of the war. From there he would continue on to the Mexican border or strike west for California or Oregon.

Buckner came to attention. A man and a woman had come out of the general store and appeared to be headed for the bank. They could complicate matters, cause a delay as the day was growing old and Grovertown's inhabitants would soon be out and moving along the street going about their daily lives. That posed the possibility of an encounter as he made his escape—one thing he had hoped to avoid.

Tension drained from his lank body. The pair turned away and were now headed for the restaurant next to the Missouri Hotel. There were now three more persons on the street, he noted as he watched the pair enter the eating establishment. He shook his head impatiently. Drawing the thick, nickel-plated watch from a pocket in his black leather vest, he consulted the Roman numerals on its face. According to the schedule there were still a few minutes until the stage was due to arrive. Restoring the timepiece to its place, he settled back to wait. If the coach was behind time resulting in Grovertown's citizenry all being up and about, robbing the bank would not be as easy as he had figured.

The day was going to be a hot one. Buckner could feel that now. He'd forgotten just how stifling hot southern Missouri could be while he was away during the war years, and later when he'd spent his time drifting about the country waiting for the railroad to pay him off.

That had come about while he was in the Army, a member of Merrill's Infantry attached to the forces of General E. B. Brown where he served as a dispatch rider until the conflict ended. Returning home, he found the railroad had built a spur line diagonally across his eighty-acre farm after diverting the creek that he depended on for water—both activities effectively making the property useless for farming.

He had protested to the heads of the railroad and they agreed that a settlement was due him. The press of war had compelled them to act without his consent or knowledge, they said, and to square it with him they were willing to pay five thousand dollars. War weary and in no mood or condition to haggle, John Buckner had agreed, directing the negotiators to forward the specified amount to him in care of C. W. Pruitt, Bank of Southern Missouri, Grovertown, at which time he would surrender a property deed and any other papers that were necessary. That was five years ago, and the five thousand earmarked by the railroad officials for the purchase had never arrived.

At first their failure to live up to the agreement and pay him his due did not trouble John Buckner. After all the years he'd spent in the war the last thing he wanted was to be tied down. Accordingly he made arrangements with C. W. Pruitt to receive and hold the money for him while he had a look at the rest of the country—all that lay west of the Mississippi.

The time eventually came when, trail weary, he headed back to Grovertown to pick up his money and settle down on a small ranch in Texas or New Mexico, raise horses and a few cattle, and enjoy himself. He was still young—a year short of thirty—and a life of comparative ease lay ahead of him.

Trouble met him head on when he went to Pruitt's bank to collect his money. There was none. The railroad had never come through. A series of changes in management was apparently delaying the payoff. For five years? Buckner had checked into the hotel to give that thought and decide what he should do. The more he mulled it over the more evident it became to him that the railroad was shirking its responsibilities and intentionally backing down on its promise. There was but one answer to that—he'd have to take matters into his own hands if he were to ever get the money due him. He knew he could expect no help from the government as it was a time when everything was being done to encourage the expansion of the rail systems.

For a full month he studied the problem, learning all he could about the coming and going of trains and their subsidiary stagecoach lines, the times of their arrivals in Grovertown, and, most important, when there was the largest amount of money belonging to the railroad on hand in the bank. To that information he added when and how a safe escape could be made once he had the money in his possession. When he had all the answers firmly set in his mind, he'd make his move.

That time was now at hand. John glanced again at his watch. The stagecoach was late by almost ten minutes.

Again returning the timepiece to his pocket, he uncon-
sciously touched the butt of the six-gun hanging at his side
and looked toward the road. Tall, a solid 175 pounds in a
muscular body, he gave the appearance of a man knowing
exactly what he was doing and determined to brook no
opposition in the accomplishing. He had dark features,
narrow eyes, near black hair, a hard, square-cut face, and
long lips partly covered by a mustache. To anyone not
knowing him he seemed to be nothing more than a cattle
buyer or grain dealer in town on business.

Buckner snapped alert as the hammer of horses' hooves
and the rattle and creaking of the oncoming stagecoach
reached him. A moment later, in a swirl of yellow dust, the
rig rounded the old, abandoned livery stable at the edge of
the settlement and swung into view. The driver, shouting
at his lathered four-up, began to slant toward the bank. In
that same moment the firm's owner opened the door and
stepped out onto the sidewalk.

When the coach was abreast of the banker the jehu
slowed his team, and leaning over, tossed down a small
black satchel containing the cash fares from various stagecoach depots as well as those collected by points along the
railroad who preferred to dispatch their collections to the
company's central office by this usually faster method.

"Howdy, Mr. Pruitt," the coach driver called, grinning
as the banker made a one-handed catch.

Pruitt nodded, watched briefly as the stage hurried on
down the street for the line's depot, and then wheeling, re-
entered the bank.

Buckner, ready, rode out two or three minutes allowing
the banker to get inside and settle at his desk. Then, again
giving his weapon a reassuring touch, and throwing a final
glance at Grovertown's still almost deserted street, stepped
out of the shadows and moved toward the entrance to the
bank.

TWO

REACHING THE DOOR of the bank, Buckner tripped the thumb latch and stepped inside quickly. After closing the solid panel he slid the bolt into place, thereby securing it, then, gun in hand, came about to face the two men he expected to be in back of the counter.

A low curse slipped from his lips. There was a third man present—Henry Guzman, the railroad detective. Squat, elderly, ruddy complected, he was dressed as he had been the last time John had seen him, in a rumpled gray suit and vest, light blue shirt the color of his eyes, and a faded, weather-stained Homburg hat. His jaw sagged when he saw Buckner. He started to rise and his hand dropped toward the bulge in his coat pocket.

"Don't!" Buckner snapped, shifting the muzzle of his .44 to cover the railroad lawman. "I don't want any killing."

"Wouldn't be nothing new to a shootist like you," Guzman muttered, and settled back in his chair.

The young clerk standing behind the wire fronting the teller's cage glanced questioningly about while Pruitt, the bank's owner, rose slowly to his feet. His sallow features were strained, his small, dark eyes wide with shock.

"John, you—you aiming to rob my bank?"

Buckner shook his head. "Not the way of it. I just come

for what's owed me. Figures up to—" He paused as someone rattled the front door, knocked, and finally moved on. "Come to something over five thousand dollars, counting interest. That's what the railroad agreed to pay me—you know that."

Pruitt said, "I expect I do, but—"

"My place was worth more, and if I hadn't been away fighting the war they'd never gotten by with it."

"That don't cut any hay," Guzman said, his features hard set and angry. "You take any money at the point of a gun, it'll be robbery. Means I'll have to track you down and get it back."

"I reckon you can try," Buckner said quietly. "Money was supposed to be turned over to Pruitt here years ago and held in trust for me. I'm here to get it."

"Still a robbery," the detective said stubbornly in his accented voice.

"Hell, I don't aim to argue with you," Buckner said, impatience sharpening his words. Swinging his attention to Pruitt, he said, "I've got my property deed with me, all made out and ready to hand over to you. Now, count out five thousand dollars in bills. Take it out of that satchel that's got the railroad's money in it."

"Now, hold on!" Guzman began, starting again to rise. "You can't do that—"

"The hell I can't," Buckner snarled, once more threatening the detective with his gun. "You keep watching me—and if you reach for that gun in your pocket again I'll take it out and bend the barrel over your head. Start counting out my money, Pruitt. When you're done you can put my deed in the satchel to show where it went. I'll forget about the interest they owe me."

The banker nodded to the man in the teller's cage. "Do what he says, Asa."

The young clerk turned to the satchel, placed it on the

counter in front of him, opened it, and began to count out the specified amount of currency. Watching him closely, Buckner moved to the gate in the counter and entered the enclosed area.

"Don't make any mistake in your figuring or I'll be back," he warned, crossing to where Guzman sat.

The clerk nodded hurriedly. "No sir. I sure won't," He glanced at Pruitt. "I'm not certain there's five thousand here."

"The railroad can borrow what you need from the bank," Buckner said dryly as he halted beside the detective. "That gun in your pocket makes me sort of nervous. Hand it over, real careful like—and butt forward."

Guzman, anger distorting his florid face, stirred slightly. He reached into a side pocket of his coat and slowly produced a nickel-plated revolver.

"I'll track you down for this," he muttered as he passed the weapon to John. "You've got the top hand now but I guarantee you it won't be for long!"

"Maybe so," Buckner replied, taking the gun and thrusting it under his belt. "You about done?" he added, turning to the clerk.

"Yes sir, just about," the man called Asa answered. "Sure a lot of bills. What're you putting them in?"

"Use one of your bank sacks," Buckner said. "Leave out about a hundred dollars. I'll be needing spending money."

"Yes sir," Asa said, and laid the requested amount to one side. "Here it is."

Again someone rapped on the front door. It had taken more time than he had figured, Buckner realized as he reached into his shirt pocket and produced a folded bit of paper.

"Here's the deed," he said, handing the document to Pruitt. "Railroad got a bargain. My place was worth more 'n five thousand dollars."

"Was what you agreed to," the banker said with a shrug.

"Sure, after it was all cut and dried. I was off fighting the war and wasn't around to do any dickering—and you good townspeople were so damned anxious to please the railroad and make it easy for them to get right of way that you never thought twice about stealing a man's property."

"Not exactly how it was—"

"It's how it looks to me and all the other men who had it done to them while they were busy keeping the Rebs off your neck. What's more, I expect the railroad was hoping I'd catch a bullet in my head so's they wouldn't have to pay for the property at all."

"It was everybody's patriotic duty to see that the railroads were able to extend their lines and help the country—"

"I've heard all that," Buckner snapped, casting a glance through the window to the street. He was wasting time. He should be on his horse and on his way out of town. "What about all the men like myself that got euchered out of their land? Don't you think they should have been considered?"

"Sure, John, but—"

"While we were being shot at and some of us killed, don't you figure that being patriotic?"

"Of course, and I can understand just how you feel—"

"I doubt that, Mister Banker. All you thought of was keeping the railroad coming and what it meant to this town, and helping it grow."

"I'm not the only one wanting that—"

"Not saying you were, but you sure could have had a mite of consideration for the soldiers out doing the fighting and keeping the Rebs and outfits like Quantrill's from taking over the town. Asa, you about got that money counted out?" Buckner glanced again to the street.

"Yes sir, all stored away in this bag."

The clerk held up a middle-size canvas sack that bore the name of the bank on it in black lettering.

"Bring it over here to me," Buckner directed. "The hundred you put aside, too." He was taking no chances on Henry Guzman, always a dangerous man, he recalled, making a move to overpower him. Nor could Pruitt be ruled out when it came to making such an attempt.

Stuffing the bag inside his shirt and pocketing the spare bills, he motioned toward a door in the back of the room. "That's a closet, I remember—"

None of the three men gave an answer. Buckner grinned. "I reckon it still is. On your feet," he continued harshly to Guzman and the banker. "Want your hands over your head where I can see them. Asa, open that closet door. All three of you are getting inside."

The clerk complied at once. Pruitt acted more leisurely as did the glowering Guzman. As he passed into the small, dark cubicle cluttered with clothing, brooms, buckets and such articles, he halted briefly.

"Telling you again, Buckner—you won't get away with this! I'll have you in leg irons and handcuffs before noon!"

Bucker shrugged. "You've sure got the right to try," he said, and slammed the door shut.

There was no key in the lock. Looking about, he seized one of the straight-backed chairs placed around a table, used, he supposed, for meetings. He dragged it up to the door and wedged it under the knob. Briefly testing it and finding it effectively blocked opening the panel at least for a while, he turned toward the rear entrance to the building. That the men would not remain prisoners for long, he knew—Henry Guzman would see to that.

Reaching the back door, Buckner removed the drop bar from its brackets and tossed it to one side. The men in the closet were already pounding and yelling, hoping to attract the attention of someone outside on the walk. Most likely their efforts would be in vain, Buckner thought; their one chance was to break down the light panel.

Moving fast, Buckner jerked open the back door that led into the alleyway running along the rear of the structures on that side of the street. Two small boys were playing under a tree a dozen yards or so down the way, and in the yard of a nearby house a woman was singing "Bonnie Blue Flag" in a quavering voice as she hung out her washing.

There was no one else in sight. Laying Guzman's gun on a close-by table, Buckner stepped out into the steadily warming day. He closed the door behind him, turned sharp left and walked along the alley until he came to the cross street. There he paused, and again took stock of his surroundings. The town's business area lay to the south. Only a scatter of residences were ahead, to the north, all seemingly deserted except for a man and woman working in a small vegetable garden fronting their white clapboard house.

Off to the east a locomotive whistled to announce its coming. If it was the train that would carry the money receipts to the principal railroad office in St. Louis, the officials there had a surprise awaiting them, Buckner thought, smiling.

After crossing the street in restrained haste, he reached the park where he had left his horse. There had been no sounds of commotion back in the direction of the bank, so he assumed the three men were still locked in the closet. Collecting his money had been amazingly easy despite the unexpected presence of Henry Guzman, but he knew the detective by reputation from years back. He was a hard, bulldog type of a man; he wouldn't remain in the closet for long, and as soon as he was out he could be counted on to form a posse and give chase.

And a hot chase it likely would be, John realized. At least it would be until they reached the Missouri-Indian Territory border. Once that was behind him and the panhandle area frequented by outlaws and known as No Man's Land, because no Territory or law agency would accept responsibility for the arid strip, became available to him, he'd have no trouble shaking the railroad detective and his posse off his trail.

He looked ahead. The sorrel gelding given to him by Colonel Merrill at the end of the war as a personal gift was standing slack-hipped in the cluster of trees where he'd tethered him. Increasing his steps, Buckner reached the big red horse, freed the rope tying him to one of the saplings, and swung up into the saddle.

Glancing back to the town and seeing that all was still quiet and normal, he raked the sorrel with his spurs, pointed the horse west, and rode off at a fast lope.

THREE

HENRY GUZMAN pulled his sweat-soaked horse to a stop on a ridge skirting a string of low hills. The black gelding was blowing hard from the steady lope the detective had held him to since early morning.

"What's the matter?" Dave Horn, one of the posse members, asked as he drew up beside him.

Guzman considered the town's general store owner coldly. He'd been dealt a hell of a poor hand insofar as posses went. There was Charlie Hanson, a farmer who had just happened to be in the livery stable when the party was being recruited, and was interested only in the three dollars a day he'd be paid. Asa Simmons, the still wet-behind-the-ears bank clerk, had been ordered to volunteer by his boss, C. W. Pruitt. Next was Pete Carstairs, the railroad agent who felt that since he was an employee of the line it was his bound duty to participate in bringing the outlaw to justice. Also along was Jim McKinley, the stage depot owner. Like Horn he probably hadn't forked a horse in months, or maybe even years. Last and probably the most reliable of the party, was Dub Trevitt, a ranch hand said to be an expert tracker and fast with a gun.

"I expect we better rest the horses a bit or we'll find

ourselves afoot," Guzman said, digging into the left pocket of his saddlebags for his telescope.

"Was you that set the pace," Horn said acidly, mopping at his face with a red bandanna. "You see anything?" He watched the detective sweep the countryside with the brass-fitted glass.

"Nope," Guzman mumbled.

Except for Trevitt he reckoned he might as well be alone. Posses were usually a very sorry thing at best, and with the one he'd been able to put together—on short notice he had to admit—he'd about scraped the bottom of the barrel. Half turning, he lowered the telescope and glanced at the men ranged about him. Hanson, the farmer, was gnawing the corner off a plug of tobacco as he slumped in his saddle.

"Couldn't you have found something better to ride than a damned white horse?" the detective demanded irritably. "Expect he can be spotted from a mile off!"

"Reckon you're right," Hanson said mildly. Clad in tattered old, blue, bib overalls, linsey-woolsey shirt, sodbuster shoes, and a ragged brim straw hat, he was carrying a double-barreled shotgun. "I'll sort of keep him around behind everybody."

Guzman supposed he had no one but himself to blame for the quality of the posse. The trouble was there simply hadn't been enough time to be selective. Besides, the town marshal had been off fishing and the sheriff had gone to Jeff City on business of some sort, leaving it all up to him. If he'd spent a lot of time picking and choosing it would have been noon or after before he'd gotten underway, and John Buckner would have had about a half day's start on him.

Capturing Buckner was important. The word had come down that the new management of the railroad had some big changes in mind—among them the retirement of employees who were beyond what they considered a "vigorous" age. That meant but one thing; they intended to cut loose all men they figured were too old to do a job and consign them to living, or existing, on what they termed a pension.

It was rumored his name was on the list of those being considered as no longer fit. Such was a bitter pill to swallow for a man like Henry Guzman. He'd been faithful to the line for twenty years more or less, and while he admittedly had reached the age of threescore and a half, he was still able to do his job, and do it a damned sight better than some of those ragpickers and joy-boys he'd seen them talking to. It would seem that experience and loyalty to the company didn't count for a pound of feathers with the higher-ups. All they thought about was hiring on younger men who they could get for less money.

Well, he'd show them that experience was worth plenty, that age didn't figure into it at all if a man was able to do his job well—and that's just what he'd do! He'd bring in John Buckner, and he'd do it before the damned outlaw had time to spend a dime of the five thousand dollars he'd stolen from the railroad. They'd sure think twice about turning him loose then, and—

"Mr. Guzman—"

Dub Trevitt's low, calm voice cut in on the detective's thoughts. Guzman turned to look at the cowhand, shadowed under a wide-brimmed hat and wearing a faded blue army shirt, dark pants, knee-high boots, red neckerchief, and two holstered revolvers about his slim waist. A rifle slung in its leather from his saddle and a long-bladed Green River knife hung from his belt.

"Yeh?"

"I seen something moving along them trees, 'way over yonder to the right," Dub said. "Maybe if you'd look through that glass of your'n you could tell if it was him."

"Hell, he wouldn't have gone that way!" Carstairs, a tall, gaunt man in a gray suit, hat, and tan duster, said. "That'd take him right straight into Indian country—and he ain't that big a fool. My guess is he lit out south for Arkansas and then—"

"It's him," Guzman cut in, holding the glass steady on the distant figure. "He's doing just what you're claiming he wouldn't do."

"Well, then, he's a plain damn fool," Carstairs said, loosening his tie and collar. "He won't get five miles before they'll have his scalp."

"I thought all the tribes in the Territory were friendly," Asa Simmons said, frowning. Like Carstairs, he hadn't had time to change clothing, and was also wearing a gray suit, ordinary hat, and a duster. Young, in his early twenties, he was a slender, dark-eyed man not too comfortable in the role of a posse member, and was there only because C. W. Pruitt had insisted.

"Ain't nobody ever got around to telling them all they was supposed to be friendly," Carstairs said dryly. "Being hostile is just the nature of a redskin. Can say this, if we go on into the Territory after Buckner, we're going to have to keep our eyes peeled or we'll sure lose our hair."

Simmons shifted nervously on his saddle, and glanced off into the distance. His expression was troubled. "I've never had to shoot anybody. Wasn't in the war."

"Good chance you won't have to now—Indian or otherwise," Dave Horn said. "Don't pay no mind to Pete. He likes to scare folks. What do you think, Henry? It for certain you're looking at Buckner?"

"For certain," the detective replied.

"Which way do you think he's headed? Into the Territory or maybe west?" Dave Horn asked. The merchant was a heavy-set dark-faced man. He wore part of a dusty blue serge suit, a round, low-crowned brown hat and a yellow duster. The rifle he carried under one arm was obviously new, and possibly had been borrowed from store stock.

"He's running west," the detective said in his short, clipped way. He cast a glance upward to the sky where clouds were gathering. "Damn it to hell, going to rain for sure."

"What if he makes it to the Colorado or New Mexico border?" Jim McKinley wondered. "Won't we have to pull up there? We ain't got no authority once we're out of Missouri."

"I've got all I need," Guzman snapped.

"That mean you been deputized to go into any other state or territory if you need to?" Carstairs asked, tightening his grip on the reins as his restless horse began to shy about.

"I go wherever my job as a railroad detective takes me."

"The railroad sure don't go into Colorado or New Mexico," McKinley said.

He was a short, red-faced man in a black sateen shirt, denim pants and Hyer boots. A wide-brimmed straw hat was on his head, and a stained gray scarf was about his neck. Unlike some of the others he was not wearing a duster, had instead a slicker tied behind the cantle of his saddle.

"That don't make a damn to me!" Guzman snarled. "I ain't letting Buckner get away."

"Well, I still think we should've waited for the marshal," McKinley grumbled. "He would've at least had some authority, in case we need it."

"Now, if that's how you all feel, you can turn back right now!" Guzman snapped, and digging spurs into the black, started down off the ridge at a run.

Guzman didn't bother to turn and see if McKinley and the others were following. If they chose to return to Grovertown it would be fine with him; he didn't need those bellyaching counter-jumpers, he could nail John Buckner by himself.

But when Guzman did look back, as he reached the foot of the slope and was riding out onto a wide flat that separated the red hills from the distant trees into which Buckner had disappeared, he saw that all six members of the posse were still with him.

FOUR

BUCKNER felt the first drop of rain as he was entering a small grove of pin oaks. The sky, clear when he had ridden out of Grovertown, had quietly clouded until it was now thickly overcast.

It didn't matter to him. He figured he had left the settlement unnoticed, and further, he could bank on a half hour or possibly a full hour before the man he had to worry about—Henry Guzman—and the others broke out of their closet prison and got underway.

Of course, it was still a long ride to the Missouri-Indian Territory border and he would be well on his way there by the time Guzman and the posse he was certain to raise could be on his trail after figuring out which way he had gone. And if the rain continued it would wipe out all signs of his passage, which would mean he could forget all about the railroad detective and the riders he'd have with him.

The trees and shrubbery all about him began to resound with the hard patter of raindrops, and the good smell of wet sumac and pines began to fill the air. Shortly the storm increased and Buckner, casting about for shelter, pulled up in a shallow coulee fronting a low bluff. The slanting rain appeared to be coming from the southeast, and while the

ragged lee side of the formation had no overhang, it sheltered him to some extent.

Despite the fact he was now thoroughly wet, he pulled
his slicker from its place on his saddle, shook the folds out
of it, and drew it on. It was sort of like closing the hen-
house door after the fox had been there, he told himself
wryly, recalling an old expression of his father's.

It had been a good, if hard, life in those days, working
the farm with his father. They'd gotten along well, and the
log house beneath a spreading black walnut tree was always
pleasant no matter how deep the snow or hot the sun.

John didn't remember much about his mother. She had
died while he was little more than a toddler, and for a while
an aunt had come to live with them and help with his up-
bringing, but eventually she left, fated to go on, as was the
custom for maiden aunts, to see to the welfare of another
needy relative, this time an ailing sister.

Leaning back against the face of the bluff, Buckner drew
out cigarette papers and a muslin sack of tobacco, a habit
he had picked up during the war. The conflict had changed
everything for him. His father had died shortly after he had
heeded President Lincoln's call to arms, and it had been
necessary to turn the farm over to a family that he had
thought would make good use of it. Instead, he discovered
when he came home that they had let it go to wrack and
ruin.

It had been a pretty good little farm, not large, being
only forty acres, when he and his father ran it. The rich
Missouri soil was productive, and there was always plenty
of water from nearby Gooseberry Creek, as they had
named the stream that he and his parent had worked so
hard to create.

But none of that had counted for anything when the
railroad had moved in wanting right of way. Then, in his
absence and with the authority assumed by the government

in its overwhelming desire to encourage the extension of the iron rails, the farm became the property of the railroad, who quickly converted it all to their own use.

Actually he didn't take the loss of the farm too hard. With his father gone everything there had changed, and the longing to travel, to see the country he had spent four years fighting for, pressed him hard. Thus, shortly after his return and once he'd made arrangements with C. W. Pruitt at the bank to take care of the money due him from the railroad when it came in, he set off. Years later, weary of drifting, he had come home to collect his money and all of the interest it had earned, only to find disappointment awaiting him.

John Buckner stirred, glanced skyward. The storm seemed to have let up some but the heavy overcast still held. He'd be making a wet camp that night for sure, he thought, but that was of little consequence. He'd passed many days and nights far worse than this during his time in the Army.

He had lined up with General E. B. Brown at the Springfield, Missouri, garrison when he enlisted, hoping to be in the cavalry. He was transferred shortly, however, to the command of Colonel Lew Merrill, which happened to be infantry. Later Merrill, recognizing his wishes as well as his hopes, assigned him the duties of dispatch rider.

John spent the rest of the war with Colonel Merrill but never realized just how capable his commanding officer was until the encounter with a large Confederate force at Hartville.

They had been camped along the Gasconade River, some forty miles east of Springfield, when word came down that the garrison there was under siege by the Confederates under General Marmaduke. Worse yet General Brown had been wounded by a sniper and was in a bad way.

The command there was now in the hands of a Colonel Crabb, who was asking for all the help he could get.

Merrill responded at once, setting out for Springfield with his comparatively small contingent of infantry and artillery. Midway he ran head-on into Marmaduke with a much larger force.

Merrill reacted immediately. He ordered his men to lie down in the tall grass and make no move until given the word. They were to be ready to shoot on command. The regiment did as directed, and upon order rose as one and began to fire their weapons, the infantry making good use of their rifles, the artillery of their fieldpieces.

The Confederate advance halted abruptly, and shortly began to fall back. A second try to move forward was made, and then a third, but Merrill's well-hidden men continued to pour a deadly hail of lead into them. Finally the order came for the Confederates to retreat and they withdrew. Merrill lost eighty men but Marmaduke's casualties were much higher.

When it was over Merrill summoned Buckner. He was promoted to the rank of sergeant and was to ride at once to the garrison at Springfield, advise Colonel Crabb of the encounter with Marmaduke, and of their victory over him. That area of Missouri should now be secure for the Union, he believed.

At the end of the war Merrill, to show his sincere appreciation for the fine soldier John Buckner had been, gave him the sorrel gelding he had been riding, along with an invitation to work for him on a farm he had acquired. But Buckner, while appreciating the gift of the horse, had no wish to return to the drudgery of farming, and expressed his thanks, said farewell to Merrill and the men still with him, and headed back to Grovertown—and the several years of wandering across the land that lay ahead for him.

Now he was starting out to drift again, this time, however, with five thousand dollars stowed away in his saddle-bags, and followed by the law in the form of a tough, no-nonsense railroad detective who had the reputation of hanging on in a chase like a beaded lizard until he brought down the man he was pursuing.

Buckner brushed at the moisture on his face and pulled away from the bluff. The rain had stopped but the soft sound of water dripping steadily from the trees and off the bushes invaded the stillness. Best he not hold back any longer, he realized. It would be foolhardy to push his luck.

As far as he knew the detective had no idea of the route he had taken when he rode out of town. But Guzman just might guess right—and there was the chance someone had noticed his departure, and upon being questioned, could point the way.

Crossing to the sorrel Buckner brushed the rainwater from the saddle seat and swung up. The slicker was of some protection from the wet leather but he was already soaked to the skin and the change was hardly noticeable.

He clucked the big horse into motion, maintaining the same westerly course for the Indian Territory. He was certain how far it would be to the border between there and Missouri, but the distance separating Grovertown and the state line was about a hundred and fifty miles, he recalled. He had trimmed that down some in the five or six hours that he'd been riding.

It was still a long way, he concluded—a distance that would take another two or three days, all depending upon the terrain and the weather. If the rain continued, and the intervening creeks rose—and the dark Missouri mud thickened and became more tenacious—it would take longer.

He broke out of the trees into a string of low, rolling hills. Movement well off to his left brought him up sharply. Riders. Seven of them coming on fast. Buckner swore deeply. Digging spurs into the sorrel's flanks, he sent him rushing ahead.

It was Guzman and his men he saw as he veered the sorrel in behind a stand of brush. He didn't know how the detective had gotten on his trail so quickly—but there he was.

FIVE

"THIS HERE RAIN ain't going to make tracking easy," Pete Carstairs said as they moved off the ridge and started across the wide flat toward the trees where John Buckner had been seen.

"Ain't nothing in this world ever easy," Hanson grumbled.

Guzman made no comment. Posses were pretty much the same. They were all fired up to ride and do their bound duty for the first few hours and were ready to quit when the saddle got a bit hard.

"You figure Trevitt can track him through all this?" Dave Horn wondered.

"Hell, I don't know!" the detective snarled. "Ask him."

The storekeeper brushed at the raindrops pelting his face. His narrow-brimmed hat was of little use in the steady shower, and he was having trouble seeing.

"What about it, Dub? Ain't this rain going to wipe out any tracks he'll leave—if we have to get down to tracking?"

Trevitt, slumped in his saddle, water running off the crease in the brim of his big Texas hat, shrugged.

"Maybe. Can't tell nothing about it till we get to where we last seen him."

"It'll be a hell of a chore finding that place, I'm thinking," Hanson grumbled.

"Maybe," Trevitt replied laconically.

They rode on, the pace of their horses now down to a plodding walk as the surface of the flat had turned into hoof-deep mud. Small rivulets were beginning to flow, draining off the higher areas into shallow gullies which in turn raced to empty their roily contents into the larger arroyos.

"You figure he seen us?" McKinley wondered, shifting about on his saddle. He had donned an old poncho made from a wool army blanket, and it was shedding its collection of water at low points, drenching his legs and boots.

"Likely," Guzman said.

"Then if he did there ain't much use of us keeping after him until this storm's over, is there?"

The sounds of the horses' hoofs sinking into the mud and then being withdrawn were loud sucking noises in the wet quiet. The rain, however, had let up to some degree and was now a thinning shower.

"You think Buckner is just going to pull up and wait for us?" There was anger and impatience in Guzman's voice. "Hell no, he ain't. He'll keep right on riding till dark—maybe after that."

"Well, I sure don't cotton to the idea of looking for him in the dark," McKinley said. "I figure he would as soon put a bullet in a man as draw his next breath . . . Goddammit, Charlie—watch what you're doing! You keep bumping into—"

"Quiet back there!—and hold up."

Guzman's voice slashed through McKinley's words. The riders came to a halt. After a long minute Carstairs said, "What is it, Henry, you hear something?"

"Thought I did. A horse, maybe. Was on up ahead."

"Getting so dark, and in this rain you couldn't've seen

him if he'd been right up there on the trail ahead of us,"
Hanson said. "When we stopping, Henry?"

Asa Simmons, who had remained silent almost from the
time they had ridden out of the settlement, nodded. The
motion dumped a quantity of water trapped by the curled
brim of his hat into his lap, as they moved on.

"What I'd like to know, too, Mr. Guzman. Can't say I'm
enjoying this much. I'm not used to sitting in a saddle this
long—much less in a rainstorm. I vote for pulling up and
having a bite to eat. Last time I ate was at breakfast."

"You'll be lucky if you get some grub before morning,"
Horn said. "Ain't that right, Henry? Our next meal will
probably be at sunup—if the sun does come up."

"Hell, I'm with the boy!" McKinley said. "I'm aching all
over, cold as a well digger's ass in winter, and hungry
enough to eat my saddle. I say we stop and—"

"Keep riding," Guzman cut in sharply. "I don't know
how close we are to Buckner, but we can't be far."

"You aiming to keep us moving all night?"

"If we have to—"

"He's staying on the regular trail, Mr. Guzman," Trevitt
said. "I reckon he'll keep doing that till he gets to the
Indian country. Hard to figure what he'll do then."

"Meaning?" McKinley pressed.

"That he'll have to stop sometime, same as we will," the
cowhand replied. "Going to be too dark to travel pretty
soon. Horses could fall."

It had begun to rain harder but in the tree and brush
covered hills there was some protection from the hammer-
ing drops. "I don't see how we can build a fire if we stop,"
Simmons muttered. "Sure won't be able to find dry wood."

"That'll be a chore all right," Hanson said.

They were no longer riding single file but were now
three abreast with Dub Trevitt slightly forward. The cowhand was hunched over his chunky little buckskin, eyes

fixed straight ahead. Now and then he would bend low and, without stopping, look closely at the trail. The hoofprints of John Buckner's horse were not so evident now as the path, faint at best, was littered with last season's leaves and needles and other debris blown in by the various passing winds.

The sky had darkened quickly and daylight had come to an end and among the trees and lesser growth it was rapidly becoming impossible to see more than a horse length ahead. The storm, quiet up to then, began to make its presence known with low mutterings of thunder, and lightning slashed the northern horizon periodically.

"I reckon we best quit, Mr. Guzman," Trevitt said after his horse had slipped and all but fell on the uncertain footing. "Ain't no use crippling us an animal. If a man finds himself afoot out here he's sure in for a hard time. Anyways, I expect that fellow has had to pull up, too."

Guzman drew his white-stockinged black to a halt. For several moments he stared off into the dripping darkness ahead, and then he shrugged. Trevitt was right. To continue under such conditions would be dangerous, and not very smart—and Henry Guzman prided himself on being smart—but he wasn't convinced that what the cowhand had said about Buckner also halting was true. Maybe he would hold up for the night and maybe he wouldn't.

"All right, we'll pull up and rest a spell. But if this storm blows over, come midnight, we'll move on."

The riders promptly veered off the trail and halted in a small hollow between several low hills. There were no trees but the clearing was ringed with various shrubs all of which were dripping steadily. The rain, however, had once again stopped.

"Reckon I can scare up a little dry wood from under these here bushes," Dub Trevitt said when he had dismounted and was standing wet and shivering in the center of the clearing. "I don't figure a little bitty fire is going to be noticed by anybody."

"Sure would feel good," Carstairs said, chafing his hands to restore circulation. "I'm so goddam cold I—"

"Go ahead," Guzman cut in abruptly. "But be damn sure you keep it low."

"Sure thing, Mr. Guzman," Trevitt said, and moved off toward the brush enclosing the area.

"Guess that means we can boil up some coffee," Horn said. "I put some fresh ground in the grub sack—along with a side of bacon and some biscuits."

"Coffee'll have to do. Bacon frying can be smelled a mile away," Guzman snapped.

"But dammit all, Henry, we—"

"Later, sometime after sunup and we get an idea of where Buckner is, then it'll be time to stop and eat," the detective said in a kinder tone.

Horn said no more but began to prepare the coffee. Others went about the business of shaking out their wet clothing and endeavoring to make themselves more comfortable.

"Not sure about this rain blowing over," McKinley said, producing a quart bottle of whiskey from his saddlebags. "Here," he added, handing the bottle to Carstairs. "A swallow or two of this'll take the chill out of your bones."

The lanky Carstairs nodded, took a swig from the bottle and passèd it on to Hanson. "Sure would like something to eat," the farmer said, taking his turn. "Never had time to get anything."

"Get some of them biscuits Horn was talking about," Guzman said, taking the liquor. He downed a healthy swallow. "Some of them and coffee'll hold you for a while."

He turned to face Trevitt coming into the clearing with an armload of small branches and sticks he had dug out from under the brush. Dropping it in the center of the clearing, he glanced about.

"Where's the coffee pot? Figured one of you'd have it ready by the time I got back."

"It's ready. Don't get your dander up," Horn said, setting the fire-blackened container, already filled with water and a generous helping of ground coffee, alongside the wood. "But no bacon. Henry's afraid Buckner'll smell it frying."

"Likely," Trevitt said.

Crouching over the pile of limbs and twigs, the cowhand selected a few of the smaller pieces, couched a handful of leaves and moss in their center, and placing the nest-like arrangement to one side, thumbnailed a match into life. After laying it on the tinder he fanned the small flame into stronger life, and shortly had a fire going.

"Damn! That sure looks good!" McKinley said as Trevitt fed larger sticks to the flames. "You got a drink coming when you're done there, cowboy."

"Feels good, too," Carstairs said, warming his hands over the flames. "Set that pot in there, Dave, let's get that coffee to going."

Guzman, a few steps back, just as chilled as the other men, who were all now crowding about the fire, swore silently. They were acting like a bunch of greenhorns. Lord only knew what they'd do if it came down to a shootout with John Buckner.

It began to rain again, creating difficulty for the low fire. As the flames began to dart back and forth, sending out a hissing sound, Trevitt rose, crossed to his horse, untied the leather strings that held his blanket roll to the saddle, and separated the tarp from the woolen cover that it wrapped. Then he jammed the blanket into one of the saddlebag pockets and returned to the fire.

Holding the bit of canvas over the flickering flames, he

shielded the fire from the rain. Almost at once it took heart and began to burn more brightly. Hanson, taking a hand in the proceedings, procured four arm-length sticks from the brush and drove them into the soft ground around the flames, creating a canopy.

"Obliged," Trevitt said in his brief way, when the strain was gone from holding the tarp. "Was getting mighty tired."

The water in the pot was beginning to boil, setting up the odor of coffee soon ready. Horn got several cups from his grub sack and passed them around. As the men continued to crouch about the fire, Trevitt moved off into the brush again in search of more dry wood. Hanson and Carstairs, taking their cue from the cowhand, got their bedroll tarps and, gathering into two groups, sat, wet and miserable, hunched about the fire, the tarps held over their heads as they waited for the coffee to be ready.

Guzman joined with Simmons, McKinley and Hanson under the last's canopy. The detective had nothing to say, plainly irritated by the forced delay, and when Trevitt returned after a time with another armload of wood, he merely nodded as the cowhand, building up the fire with more fuel, spoke.

"Mr. Guzman—"

The coffee was boiling busily and Horn, removing the pot from the fire, stirred down the froth and poured a quantity into each cup.

"Just wanted to say we ain't going nowheres tonight. Can hear a lot of water running somewhere on down the way. Just wouldn't be smart. And that there Buckner won't be trying to move either unless he's dumber'n I figure he is."

Guzman was silent for a long breath. "All right, we'll stay here till daylight," he said, taking a sip of the scalding hot coffee. "Then we're moving on."

SIX

BUCKNER gazed off into the east through the misty air. Faint light was beginning to show along the hilly horizon. It wouldn't be long until daylight, he reasoned, although it would come late, thanks to the thick overcast.

He had been reluctant to halt during the night, fearing the posse under Henry Guzman's relentless determination would continue despite the persistent rain. But when traveling in the steady downpour became too treacherous he felt compelled to halt, believing the detective and the men with him would so the same.

It was the second time he would be gambling on Guzman's turn of mind, but in this instance he felt certain he was right. No sane man who cared a damn about his horse or his own neck would risk moving along on such dangerous footing in the blackness.

So he had swung off the trail, inbred caution forcing him to be circumspect, and halted in a small, shoulder-high cluster of scrub oak and junipers where he had the flat side of a butte to his back. There he spent the long night hunched against the reddish formation, blanket wrapped about his lean body and canvas poncho shedding the rain to some extent while water steadily filled the gullies and other depressions around him.

He satisfied his hunger by eating a little of the sliced roast beef and biscuits he had brought along, and while a cup of hot coffee would have done much to make the dragging hours more endurable, he passed up the idea. Finding dry wood would be no easy task, and keeping a fire going, if he dared risk the smell of smoke in the rain, would require constant attention. Best he play it safe and wait until daylight, hope the rain would stop. Then, once he felt it was safe, he could pull up and make coffee.

The storm, never a really hard downpour but a succession of heavy showers, let up when the sun made a tentative appearance in the east—showing little more than a bar of weak light that silhouetted the hilltops. But it was daylight, if gray and cold. Immediately Buckner wiped off his saddle seat once again, and settling into the wet leather, moved on. He kept parallel to the trail rather than on it as he resumed his westerly course.

One thing was definite, with a determined Guzman and his posse coming on relentlessly, he would need to find an area in which to travel where there would be good cover and he would not be easily visible. Would it be north for Colorado, or south into New Mexico? He pondered the problem as he rode on.

Around midmorning, with the sky clearing slowly, and no signs of the posse anywhere along his back trail, Buckner again pulled off into a hollow well off the path, and drew to a halt. The sorrel was in need of a few minutes rest and a bait of grain, and Buckner felt the need for something more substantial than the roast beef and biscuits he'd had earlier.

Walking to the crest of one of the hills that encircled the hollow, he made doubly certain he'd not overlooked any riders in the area, and then returned to where the sorrel waited, poured a small amount of grain into the horse's nosebag, put it in place, and began to see to his own needs.

He could hear an arroyo running full force somewhere off to his left, and the ground around him was muddy and soft from the rain. Shrubs, trees and lesser bushes were heavy with water, and by the time he had rooted out enough dry branches and twigs from beneath them he was wet again.

He gave no thought to that. Growing up and working a farm, being soaked to the skin from rain and chilled to the bone by snow and winter winds was no new experience. Add to that his time in the Army, and little in the way of inclement weather fazed him.

He had no trouble getting a fire started, having found some paper along with his box of matches in his saddlebags, and in short order had the lard tin he carried for such purpose balanced on rocks over the flames, filled with water and ready for the crushed coffee beans.

He ate quickly, consuming a fairly large quantity of warmed-over beef, biscuits, a can of peaches, and two cups of coffee with the thought that the meal might have to last him until dark or perhaps later if he discovered Guzman and the posse anywhere in the vicinity.

When the meal was finished he stored the utensils in one of the grub sacks, removed the nosebag from the sorrel and returned it to his saddlebags, then once again climbed the hill to search for the posse.

There was still no sign, and that set up a faint worry within him. He would feel much better if he knew where Guzman and the six riders were. It was far too easy to blunder into them when traveling blind—but he couldn't waste time lamenting the fact. He'd move on, get his bearings when he got nearer to the Indian Territory, and then, depending on where Guzman was, decide which way to go. There was a slim possibility that the detective and his men had taken a wrong trail, which would account for their not being seen. But John Buckner put no real faith in that.

Returning to the clearing near the bluff, he mounted the sorrel and pushed on making his way as fast as possible through the wet shrubs and over the mud-slick ground, angling finally back to the trail. Every now and then he would pull to a stop and listen for sounds that would tell him that Guzman and his men were close, but each time he could hear only the dripping of the trees and brush. Off in the distance a meadowlark was whistling vigorously as if trying his best to brighten up the sullen day.

By noon the sky was clearing and only patches of dirty gray clouds were hanging around the horizon. The sorrel had made better time with no rain to face, and Buckner began to feel more confident about reaching the comparative safety of the Indian Territory by nightfall. Too, he was beginning to put more stock in the possibility that the detective had gotten off on the wrong trail.

It would be difficult to know exactly when he reached the border where Missouri ended and the Indian country began. He had been through there once or twice before while drifting about and on a single occasion when he carried a dispatch from Merrill to the officer in command of the garrison, Camp Collins on the Cache La Poudre River in Colorado.

Buckner came to an abrupt halt. A noise off to his right caught his attention. It sounded like horses, several of them. The posse? He wheeled the sorrel into a thicket of tall brush. How could Guzman and his party close in so quickly—and from that side of the trail? As far as he could figure they should be miles behind him—and to the east, unless, of course, he had underestimated the detective and he and the posse had not been halted by the rain that night.

The sound grew louder—the steady muted tunk-tunk of horses moving across the soaked ground. Buckner came off the sorrel, and crouched low, drew his .44. He didn't want it to come down to bloodshed with Guzman, or any of the posse members, but he felt he was in the right and would defend himself and his property if a showdown developed.

As well be shot for a sheep as a goat, he thought. They had a charge of bank robbery against him which Guzman and bank owner Pruitt would no doubt push to the limit; he just might as well go all out to retain possession of his five thousand dollars.

Buckner hunched lower. The riders would pass a half a dozen strides or so in front of him. Fortunately the growth in the area was thick and unless the sorrel set up a disturbance he should go unnoticed. He was in an ideal position to spring an ambush if he so desired, and the thought did enter his mind, but he brushed it away. Ambush was not his style, never was, even during the war.

The moments ticked by with aggravating slowness. John Buckner clamped his left hand over the hammer of his gun to muffle the click and cocked the weapon. If it came down to a shootout he'd be forced to open up on the nearest man, and then, during the resulting confusion, get to the sorrel and make a run for it. The trees and thick shrubs extended southward as far as his limited vision could determine, and with luck and the element of surprise on his side, he should be able to get away from what was left of the posse.

What was left of the posse. The words set up a hollow echo in his mind. Killing a man, Guzman or any of those in the posse, sent a chill traveling through him. When the war ended he thought he'd seen the last of killing, but that had not been the way of it. There had been times during his years of wandering about the frontier when it was stand or back down, and he'd never been one to do the latter. Each occasion had sickened him and caused him to vow once more to never again use his gun on a man, but here once more he faced a situation of kill or be killed, all over what was rightfully his.

The head of a horse bobbing wearily up and down came into view. Buckner tensed, tightened his grip on the butt of his .44. The neck of the animal appeared—and then the rider. Buckner eased back. He swore softly. It wasn't Guzman or any of the posse but an Indian. The brave was hunched forward, his back a dull copper in the weak sunlight. A rifle lay across his legs and he looked to be dozing.

A second brave appeared, and then a third, all half asleep. Evidently it was a hunting party returning to their village after a sally into Missouri in search of game. A fourth buck rode into view, this one with a deer slung over the withers of his horse.

Buckner came to his feet as the Indians passed on unseeing. He was damned glad it hadn't been the posse. He rolled himself a cigarette, lit up and turned to the sorrel. Mounting, he moved on. He wasn't far from the Indian Territory now, that was certain. He should make it by dark.

SEVEN

"COME ON, come on, let's move out!" Henry Guzman said peevishly.

He was settled in the saddle on the black he was riding, and had been ready to resume the pursuit of John Buckner for a good ten minutes. The party had spent a miserable night in the deep brush, the wet and cold alleviated only by the warmed-over meat and whiskey-laced coffee they had consumed. Shaking his head at the aggravating slowness of the posse members, he brushed at his mustache impatiently.

"The man'll be clear over in the Red River country by the time we get started! Hurry it up!"

McKinley, in the process of tying down his blanket roll, paused. He glanced at Hanson, his ordinarily ruddy features pale and drawn from weariness.

"Want to talk a mite to you, Henry."

The detective stiffened. The lines around his mouth hardened, and a look of resignation came into his faded blue eyes as if he knew in advance what the stagecoach agent intended to say.

"All right, spit it out. I'm listening."

"Well, me and Charlie have been talking this over, Henry. We've got to go back. The station can't run for long without me—just can't depend on that hostler I've got working for me to see to everything. Lose my shirt if I did. And Charlie says the chores on his farm are piling up, and he needs to be looking after them."

Guzman stared off into the dripping trees and swore deeply. The rain had stopped hours ago but everything was wet, and he knew that despite all the protective measures he had taken, he'd be soaked to the skin within an hour.

"Figured this would be coming up," he snapped. "Now you both listen to me—you hired on for as long as it took to bring in Buckner, and we ain't done that yet."

"We realize that, Henry, but we didn't think it'd take more'n yesterday to do it. And now, getting all this here rain, it's certain to wash out Buckner's tracks so's we'll for sure lose him."

"Don't fret none about that," Guzman said irritably. The men, except for McKinley, were all mounted and ready to go, finally, but here he was faced with this further delay. "That's Trevitt's job—unless he's quitting, too."

The cowhand, cupping his hands about the match he was holding to a slim, brown paper cigarette, shook his head slightly. He looked at Guzman from under the soggy, limp brim of his big hat.

"It's this way with me, Sheriff," he drawled, "long as you're paying, I'm staying."

"I'm not the sheriff!" Guzman shot back angrily. "And staying with me is what I'm expecting from all of you."

Somewhere off in the trees a rain bird uttered its harsh, forlorn call. The men listened silently, and then after a few moments Carstairs stirred.

"Reckon me and Horn are up against the same problem, Henry," he said, removing the unlit briar pipe from his mouth. "And I know this is railroad business but I best get back to the station and be taking care of that end of it."

"Same here," Horn said. "My missus can't run the store

all by herself, and our boys are too little to be of much help."

Henry Guzman exploded abruptly. "Goddammit—why don't you all just turn around right now and hightail it for home! I can run this bastard down by myself. I've done it before, I can do it again!"

"You best not be forgetting me," Trevitt said quietly.

"Or me," Asa Simmons added. He had weathered the night much better than the others, thanks to his youth. "Mr. Pruitt told me to stick with you till we got the money back, and that's what I aim to do."

"It's up to you," the detective said stiffly, and put his hard gaze on McKinley and Hanson. "You just as well pull out right now."

"Well, no, Henry, we sort of figured to stay with you till noon. Then, if it's all right, we'll turn back. We just might jump Buckner by then."

"What about you and Horn?" Guzman demanded, shifting his angry attention to Carstairs.

"We'll stick with it until tomorrow morning," the railroad agent replied. "If we haven't caught up with him by then, Dave and me'll have to go back." The rain bird called out again. At the cuckoo's warning Pete Carstairs glanced to the sky, now a murky blue. "Storm ain't over yet, that's for sure."

Guzman shrugged. More rain couldn't make things much worse, he thought. Somewhere out in far southwest Missouri, or maybe in Indian Territory, with his posse falling apart he'd have a hell of a time getting his job done— but he would even if the pair who declared they'd stay with him changed their minds! Not one of them knew how important it was to him personally to overtake John Buckner and recover the money the outlaw had so brazenly stolen right from under his nose—and he'd be damned if he'd humble himself and tell them. It shouldn't be necessary anyway. They all ought to have enough respect for the law to want Buckner caught and jailed for the crime he had committed.

"Well, we've done enough jawing," the detective said abruptly. "I've got to get moving. All of you can do what you damn please far as I'm concerned. Just head back when you get the notion." He paused, looked at the cowhand. "All right, Trevitt, let's pick up his trail."

Dub nodded, tossed the limp butt of his cigarette aside. Wordless, he raked his horse with spurs and sent him moving away from the others into the general direction of the path they had been following. The sun was out now and its warming rays were struggling to make themselves felt.

"I sure do hate having to leave you, Henry," McKinley said, settling in his saddle. "But I just plain ain't got no choice."

Guzman made no reply, simply fell in behind Dub Trevitt and rode on. The cowhand-tracker led them onto the main trail in very few minutes, and picked up signs of Buckner's passage within the first hour. Several times he moved out ahead of the party—taking a second look, he termed it—and each time he returned to advise he had seen no rider ahead but that he was certain from other indications that Buckner was still in front of them, following the established path.

This disturbed Henry Guzman somewhat. Why would Buckner be sticking to the main trail, thereby leaving signs of his passage for the posse to find so easily? Why wouldn't an outlaw attempting to escape the law cut away at first chance, and do his utmost to throw pursuit off his trail?

Buckner had some trick up his sleeve, the detective concluded. That was the only reasonable explanation. All well and good. Let him. As long as he left a trail or some other sign of his passing that Dub Trevitt could follow, the end would be the same. Eventually he would overtake Buckner and take him prisoner.

Guzman's thoughts came to a halt as Trevitt, returning from one of his frequent sashays ahead, kneed his horse in close to the detective.

"We got some redskin company, Mr. Guzman," he said in a low voice. "Four, maybe five from the tracks."

"Indians? That what you're saying?" Horn, riding directly behind the railroad man, asked anxiously.

Guzman raised his hand and halted the party. He would just as soon Trevitt's words had not been heard, but despite the cowhand's efforts to speak low, they had been.

"Where are they?" He put the question to Trevitt in a normal tone.

Trevitt pointed off to the left. "Just can't be sure. I was off in that direction and they was going that way. Don't know if they kept on going or maybe heard us and are circling around to head us off."

Guzman gave that consideration. Finally he made a motion with his hand and the party started forward again.

"Well there ain't much we can do but go on and keep our eyes open. Could be a party of friendlies out hunting or—"

"Or it could be some hostiles looking to take a few scalps," Carstairs cut in sourly. "Expect we're in Indian country now."

"Yeh, expect we are," Guzman said. "There'll be no talking and you all have your guns ready in case we run into them."

They rode on, quiet and on the alert. Guzman cursed silently. That was the trouble with Indians; they could come and go like a breath of wind, and they could be silent as shadows as they waited around the next clump of brush to kill you.

By noon, however, after several tense hours, they encountered no one and all were breathing easier. Jim McKinley and Charlie Hanson left the party as they had indicated, planning to swing south so as to avoid meeting with the party of braves they had so narrowly missed.

The following morning after a series of showers plagued the posse, Dave Horn and Pete Carstairs took their leave, and also headed back to Grovertown. Guzman considered their departure in grim silence as they rode off into the hazy day. When they were beyond the first bend in the trail, he swung his angry attention to Trevitt and Asa Simmons.

"This here's your last chance to turn tail and head for home. Can catch up with them if—"

"Done told you I'm staying," Trevitt cut in. "Meant it."

"You wanting to get rid of us?" Simmons asked, his voice belying the uneasiness that gripped him.

"Nope, just wanting you both to know how things stand. Got to make my plans, and I don't want you whining around wanting to pull out tonight, tomorrow or two weeks from now if we're still chasing Buckner."

Simmons rubbed at the thin stubble on his jaw. "You think it might take that long to catch him?"

"Longer, maybe," Guzman said flatly. "The job ain't finished until I've got him in irons and back in Grovertown."

Asa Simmons gave that lengthy thought and then stirred in his saddle. "Well, if that's how it's to be, I expect we best push on."

"Reckon you're right," the detective said with a faint smile. Maybe he had all the dependable help he needed after all.

EIGHT

IT WAS EASIER to follow the trail, Buckner saw quickly. Too, he could travel much faster as he didn't have to contend with the sodden brush. Too, he was relieved that the party he'd encountered was not Guzman and the posse. Had it been they and not several half-asleep Indians, a shootout likely would have evolved.

He hoped he would be able to make it to southern New Mexico or Arizona and the border, if that's the direction he eventually decided to take, without it coming down to gunplay. He had no quarrel with any of the men involved, some he might even consider friends; and Henry Guzman was only doing the job he was hired to do. To shoot down any member of the posse was the last thing Buckner wanted to do.

But when he fell to thinking about Henry Guzman it occurred to him that the detective was actually out to take from him what was rightfully his—the five thousand dollars that the railroad had agreed to pay for his land but never got around to doing. He'd fight Guzman, fight him to the death if it was necessary. A man had the right the protect his property, to hang onto what was his.

Late the next day Buckner caught sight of five riders well to the east. The distance was so great that he was unable to determine if it was Guzman and the posse or not, even with the help of his telescope. If so two of the party were missing as there should be a total of seven members including Guzman. Could it be that the detective, who certainly was coming on fast, was splitting up the posse, sending out scouting parties in an effort to locate him?

Guzman would know that he was somewhere ahead, but whether to the north or south of the trail would be a mystery to him. Whatever, assuming it was the posse, Buckner realized it meant that he would need to move faster and keep a sharp watch on both sides as well as the rear.

He rode steadily, putting in long days, often continuing into the night. He saw no more of the five riders or the Indians and there was only a splatter of rain now and then. He had no precise idea of where he was. That he was somewhere in Texas he was fairly certain, but he wouldn't know for sure until he reached a small stream called Mustang Creek.

It was a landmark for him. Once there, with his bearings established, he'd be faced with the decision that had occurred to him earlier—should he head for Colorado or turn into the opposite direction, enter New Mexico and thereby follow the original route he had mapped for an escape?

It depended upon Henry Guzman. If the detective and his men continued to gain on him he would need to react quickly. To the north Colorado offered towering, thickly forested mountains along with deep canyons in which he could hide—but that was many miles away while New Mexico would be only a day's ride west.

Once there he could veer south for the Canadian, another river with which he was familiar. From there it was only one more day in the saddle to the Pecos, where he could turn his face to the sunset and ride until he came to the Rio Grande. Following its wide, placid course he would come to Socorro, the settlement at the end of the Jornada del Muerto, where he could again head west, cross the San Augustine Flats and soon find himself in Arizona, or he could stay with the Rio and cross over into Mexico with it.

New Mexico was his best bet, Buckner decided. He could gain good cover sooner, and make it easier and safer to reach Mexico, if that was to be his eventual destination.

Clouds began to build early in the day, and the smell of rain once more filled the air. He was crossing wide, open country now and having difficulty in finding cover. The reddish hills were low and rolling, and only occasionally did he come upon a deep swale or arroyo that would prevent anyone riding across the plain, extending endlessly to the east, from seeing him.

Since such slashes and depressions in the broad country were few and far between, there being only small gullies, he found himself wishing he were nearer the tailing end of the Rocky Mountains which extended down into New Mexico. There his chances for eluding Guzman would be much better.

It occurred to him as the sorrel plodded wearily along that he could cut sharp right and head north into the panhandle of the Indian Territory—a lengthy strip of desolation known as No Man's Land. A haven for outlaws, it lay like an oblong barrier between Texas on one side and Kansas and Colorado on the other—neither of which claimed or desired any legal jurisdiction over it.

Under usual circumstances a man fleeing from authority could find safety there, but Buckner was dealing with Henry Guzman, and if he ran true to form, boundaries would mean nothing to him unless it was a foreign area such as Canada or Mexico. Here Guzman would no doubt track him into the lawless strip, and from what Buckner could recall of that part of the country the opportunity for getting the railroad detective off his trail would not only be harder due to the flat terrain, but it would take him into the exact opposite direction to where he believed he would find safety. Too, riding into a nest of desperate outlaws and killers with five thousand dollars in his saddlebags would be tempting fate.

Rain began to fall shortly after noon but only in brief showers that somewhat relieved the heat that had begun to make itself felt. Several times when he located a ridge or hilltop that afforded a better view of the country behind him, he paused to rest the sorrel and throw a long, searching look at his back trail.

Once he spotted three riders moving southwest, but as before, they were too far in the distance to tell anything about them, not even the color of their horses. To him they were only dark blurs on the horizon. He was certain it was not the posse, however. Guzman had six men riding with him, and it was inconceivable that four could have pulled out so soon and left the detective with only two men to side him.

The rain continued sporadically for the rest of that day and ceased only when the soggy clouds masked the sun's descent behind the range of craggy mountains to the west.

Worn, hungry, and with no indication of the posse in any direction, Buckner drew the sorrel to a halt beneath a small cottonwood tree growing in a buffalo wallow near a row of wet, dark faded bluffs. The sorrel was as played out as he, and after picketing the big horse near the cottonwood, Buckner poured a measure of grain from his diminishing supply onto a patch of grass in front of the sorrel, then turned to his own needs.

First laying out his tarp and blanket for the night's sleep, he then rustled up a small quantity of dry wood from beneath the cottonwood and scrub growth nearby, built a low fire, boiled up some coffee, warmed a few of the biscuits and topped the meal off with a bit of the meat he had left. He was getting low on food, he realized, and it would soon be necessary to find a town where he could restock his grub sack.

Later, with the fire little more than a glow, and coyotes tuning up in the distance, he filled his cup with the last of the strong brew, and rising, walked a few steps from the camp, his attention on the sky to the south where a few stars were visible.

Standing there in the half dark, he wasn't much to look at. His clothing—blue army shirt, red neckerchief, and faded brown pants soaked by continuing rainstorms, and then dried by successive if brief sunny days—hung limply from his wide-shouldered frame. The brim of his flat crowned, plainsman style black hat dipped and sagged and his already scarred boots were coated with red mud.

Only the rugged character of his features, the lower part now bearing a growth of whiskers, appeared unchanged. The same resolute determination showed in the angles of his hard-cut face and dark eyes making it clear to all that what was his, was his, and would remain so. Finishing off the coffee, he rolled a cigarette, smoked it down to a mere stub, and shortly thereafter crawled into his blanket.

The night passed without interruption other than a visit from a pair of hungry coyotes. Attracted by the smell of the meat he had warmed, they slunk cautiously into the camp, but catching the odor of man, turned quickly and vanished into the darkness. He was up and on his way after again making coffee and completing a breakfast of meat and biscuits, which he highlighted with a can of peaches, well before the sun began to climb into a red sky.

For some reason he felt better—probably because it appeared he had shaken Guzman and the posse off his heels, and could now ride on to where he would finally come to the Rio Grande and follow it southward.

The cloudy day went by with no signs of the posse. The rain continued to hold off, and taking advantage of the coolness and the gentle nature of the terrain, Buckner pushed the sorrel hard. The sooner he reached New Mexico and lost himself in its broad, thinly populated miles, the better he would feel.

Late in the afternoon relief surged through him when he topped out a fair hill and saw a twisting sparkle of water in the far distance cutting across the rolling flats. Mustang Creek. It was a welcome sight, and after a last look at the country behind him, he urged the sorrel down the slope and rode to the stream. Narrow though it might be, he waded the big horse to its far side, adhering to the old warning faithfully observed by experienced travelers that when coming to a river however small, cross to its yonder side before making camp, as a man never knew what the night might bring. It was a wise precaution Buckner never failed to heed. Too many times he had seen a wagon-width creek turn into a raging torrent from a storm miles upstream.

He had just pulled to a halt and had swung down from the sorrel when a rattle of gunshots broke the afternoon's hush. The sound came from beyond a hill a short distance on ahead, and was a continuing cracking of pistols, rifles, and the occasional boom of a shotgun. Buckner frowned. It could be Indians or possibly outlaws down from No Man's Land not far to the north, attacking a party of pilgrims. At any rate he had no choice but to see what it was all about and lend a hand if necessary.

Going back into the saddle, he shifted the holstered .44 on his hip to a more convenient position, assured himself that his rifle was ready in the boot, and headed for the crest of the hill where he would be able to look down on whatever was taking place below.

Near the hilltop he glanced back. The three riders he'd seen earlier were just riding down into a hollow some distance to the east. They were much closer, Buckner realized.

NINE

REACHING THE RIDGE, Buckner drew the sorrel to a quick stop. Gunshots were drumming continually on the afternoon air as he looked down into a shallow valley-like area. The slope fell away from the hill where he had halted, ran on to melt into a narrow swale and then became a flat which extended to the far side. There pine trees, firs, cedars and ragged brush covered a rocky incline slanting upwards into the higher levels of a fair-sized mountain.

In the center of the swale, skidding and swaying on the muddy ground as they raced toward the trees, were two canvas-topped wagons. Riding along parallel on either side in an obvious effort to prevent the pilgrims from gaining the comparative shelter of the dense growth on the slope were four men, outlaws. They were triggering their weapons at the onrushing wagons, only one of which was now returning their fire.

Abruptly the man on the seat of the lead wagon sagged forward. The rifle he was holding slipped from his grasp and fell to the ground. Almost at the same time a shotgun in the hands of a woman crouched in front of the seat of the second vehicle laid its booming blast across the confusion of smoke and echoes.

A man and a woman attempting to hold off four outlaws!

But now the man was out of it, which left it up to the woman. Grim, Buckner threw a glance over his shoulder to the east, and then to the north. There was no sign of Guzman and the posse—but they were out there, he knew, and if he stopped to help the pilgrims he could be making it possible for the detective and his men to overtake him.

The two wagons slowed. The man lay crumpled in the arms of what was apparently his wife while the woman in the other vehicle continued firing her shotgun. He saw then that a second woman behind the seat was driving the team. The outlaws were having no difficulty in avoiding the scatter-gun's short range charge, and Buckner was certain they would not hold off much longer now. Soon they would close in, probably two from the yonder side while the remaining pair kept the woman with the shotgun busy firing and reloading. It would then be only a matter of time and it would be over.

There was movement behind the women in the canvas-arched bed of the wagon. A face appeared. Another woman! John Buckner swore. Once again he glanced over his shoulder. Still no indication of the posse. He brushed impatiently at his whiskered jaw. Hell—he had no choice but to help the women! He'd have to take his chances on Guzman catching up. He could only hope he could do what he could for the pilgrims and be on his way south before the detective rode up.

Bracing himself in the saddle, he thumbed back the hammer of his six-gun and started down the muddy slope. He'd have to leave it to the sorrel to make it to the bottom safely; he'd be plenty busy using his weapon since the odds were all against him. As he came into range he snapped a shot at the nearest of the outlaws. Smoke was drifting about the wagons and hanging in small clouds here and there in the moisture-heavy air hindering visibility somewhat, while the echoes of the gunshots seemed to also remain suspended and motionless along the floor of the swale.

The rider he had fired at, a lean, dark, bearded man wearing a tattered duster and a large, once light-colored, wide-brimmed hat, looked around startled as John's bullet grazed him. At once he cut sharp left, and yelled something to his partner a short distance behind him. Both then wheeled and started across the swale in a direct line for Buckner.

The tall Missourian grinned tightly and bent lower over the saddle. Steadying himself he leveled his weapon at the nearest rider—a narrow-faced man clad in parts of a faded army uniform. Ignoring the bullets fired randomly at him, Buckner targeted the outlaw and pressed off a shot. The man clawed frantically at the saddle horn to keep from falling, and began to pull away. The bearded man in the old duster instantly followed, and together they started to double back along the rutted floor of the swale.

Buckner threw two quick shots at the remaining outlaws, a much younger-looking man and one dressed in Mexican vaquero clothing, and, still crouching low, raced across the intervening bit of rain-soaked ground for the wagons, now halted side by side. He circled to the rear of the vehicles and pulled the sorrel to a sliding stop. Lunging from the saddle he ground-reined the horse, and making it to the near wagon in three long strides, climbed up onto the seat.

An elderly woman, moaning softly, was holding the man in her arms. One quick look told Buckner that he was dead. Reloading his gun as he hunched down behind the dashboard of the wagon, Buckner looked across to the other vehicle. The woman with the shotgun, also hunkered down between the seat and the dash, smiled tightly at him as she fed two more shells into the double-barreled weapon she was using. Behind her he could see the pale, strained features of the one doing the driving, and on beyond her, in the bed of the wagon, the third member.

The two remaining outlaws, the vaquero and the boy, had joined the retreating pair briefly, and were now returning. They were firing their weapons as they came but with much more care than earlier. The vaquero, hanging on the offside of his horse so as to offer no target at all, was triggering his gun from under the animal's neck as he rode by. The young outlaw, no more than seventeen or eighteen, Buckner judged, was crouched low on his mount, shooting as rapidly as he could thumb back the hammer and press off the trigger of the pistol he was using.

"My—my husband—he's dead."

Buckner barely heard the faltering voice of the woman sitting half on, half off the seat behind him. He looked up at her. Thin faced, mid-fifties or perhaps sixty, with light hair and grief-filled eyes, she was wearing a flowered calico dress with a bonnet made of the same cloth. Her voice had a distinct Southern accent.

"Sure am sorry," Buckner murmured for lack of something better to say as he reloaded.

"He held them off the best he could—him and Thalia. She's our eldest daughter—there in the other wagon."

John glanced at the other vehicle. It appeared to be a duplicate of the one he and the woman were in—reinforced sides, strengthened wheels and bows designed for hard, cross-country traveling.

"They for sure did," he said. "I'm wishing I could have showed up a bit sooner. Maybe your husband wouldn't—"

Buckner let the words trail off into silence. The woman wasn't listening. Besides, it was a useless thing to say. A bullet thudded into the thick side of the wagon. Buckner swung his attention to the outlaw riding by at top speed. It was the vaquero again hiding behind the body of his horse.

John fired a shot at the portion of the man's leg visible to him.

It was a difficult shot. He knew he had missed an instant after he'd triggered the .44. But he had no time to mull over the failure. The younger man had wheeled and was coming in fast. Buckner steadied himself, peered through the smoke and, leveling his gun at the oncoming rider, pressed the trigger. In that same instant the bay horse the boy was riding lurched and the bullet meant for the rider drove into its straining body. The horse seemed to wilt and abruptly collapsed.

Swearing under his breath, Buckner shifted his attention to the vaquero, once again coming back. He hated killing the outlaw's horse. It was a bit of bad luck but there was nothing to be done about it. He heard the roar of the shotgun wielded by the girl, Thalia. Her shots at the vaquero were wide as he continued to race in toward her, triggering his own weapon as he did. Off to the left the young outlaw had freed himself of his downed horse, and was waiting to be picked up by his partner.

Buckner turned his gun on the vaquero, set himself for a dead center shot. Suddenly a loud clang filled his ears. The sound seem to fill and overpower his brain completely. At the same instant a shocking blow rocked his head and turned the world around him into a void of blackness.

TEN

HURRIEDLY RELOADING the old double-barrel shot-gun for what seemed to her the hundredth time, Thalia drew back the tall, rabbit-ear hammers of the weapon. Twisting about, she aimed it at the two outlaws, now mounted on one horse and fleeing southward. She rocked back as she pulled the triggers and pain again filled her aching shoulder. As before, the shots did no good. The pellets of lead, designed for hunting rabbits and birds, showered around the outlaws with no effect.

"Are they leaving?" she heard Sibyl, her youngest sister, ask in a strained voice.

Thalia shrugged and again reloaded the shotgun. "Hard to say. The other two are waiting about a mile down the way."

"One of them's dead, I'm sure of that," Augusta, her second sister, said in a tight voice. "And Papa's hurt—maybe even dead."

Sibyl began to weep. Thalia shook her head. "Now, we don't know that for sure," she said, turning her attention to the outlaws. They were in a small group a mile or so in the distance. "We better go over and help Mama while we've got the chance . . . I'm not sure but I think that cowboy who rode in to help us got shot, too."

Augusta sighed heavily as she climbed down from the wagon. "I'm—I'm sorry we ever left Georgia! It's been nothing but hard times and trouble ever since!"

Thalia, quickly on the ground, glanced disapprovingly at her sister. "No time to talk like that, Gussie! Papa may be dead along with that cowboy—and at least three of those outlaws are still alive and hanging around!"

"But what can we do?" Augusta asked as they started across to their parents' wagon. "We can't—"

"I don't know," Thalia replied, "but I think we should all be in the same wagon. Maybe we'll have a better chance of holding them off." She paused, looked back. Sibyl, still crying, was following in her usual lackadaisical manner. "Come on, Sassy! We've got to get to Mama before those outlaws come back!"

"Papa dropped his rifle," Augusta said as they reached the wagon. "Only weapon we've got now is the shotgun."

"The cowboy was using a pistol," Thalia said. "And he's probably carrying a rifle on his saddle. They always seem to."

Thalia circled to the rear of the vehicle, allowed her sisters to climb aboard while she again threw a worried look in the direction of the outlaws. Satisfied they had not moved, she entered the wagon, hearing her mother's low, ragged voice as she did.

"Your papa's dead."

Sibyl began to weep anew. A moment later Augusta broke down as well.

Thalia was quiet for a long minute. She had loved her father very much, but grieving would have to come later. Brushing at her eyes, she said, "Crying won't help Papa now—or us. What about the cowboy?"

"He's still unconscious. I think a bullet struck him in the head," the older woman said tonelessly.

"Then we best see if we can get him fixed up so's he can

help. Those outlaws will be back—you can bet on it," Thalia said briskly. "Gussie you and Sibyl get Papa back here in the wagon. Throw a quilt over him. Mama, is the cowboy's wound bad?"

The older woman relinquished her hold on her dead husband, shook her head. "I—I don't know," she replied wearily. "He just sort of collapsed."

Thalia, leaning over the back of the crowded seat, tugged at Buckner's limp body and turned him partly over. "He's bleeding near his right temple. It doesn't look like a bullet wound—more like a cut," she said, and then, without looking up, added, "Help me get him back there, too— where we can doctor him . . . Mama, you best stay where you are—it's going to be crowded back there. You watch those outlaws. If they start coming this way, let me know."

With the help of her two sisters, Thalia dragged Buckner into the rear of the wagon and laid him out beside their father.

"Gussie, fetch the canteen of water. Sibyl, get the medicine bag," Thalia directed, ripping a bit of white cotton cloth taken from a small chest into strips as she looked more closely at Buckner's wound.

"My, isn't he a handsome one," she heard Sibyl murmur. "I hope he won't die, too."

"He just may if we don't get busy and stop the bleeding," Thalia snapped. She glanced at her mother.

Martha Alexander Tallant had aged much since they left Georgia. Her dark hair was now streaked with gray, and her eyes, once bright and sparkling, were now filled with a dullness. Her shoulders sagged and she appeared small and frail, much different from the proud, happy woman she had been at the start of the journey.

"Mama," she said gently, "will you see to the cowboy? You're so good with medicine and such. I'll just swap places with you."

Martha Tallant stirred, nodded woodenly, and with her daughter's help crawled over the seat into the back of the wagon.

Thalia, now in the front of the wagon, picked up the cowboy's revolver. It appeared to be loaded, but being unfamiliar with a handgun, she was not sure. The shotgun was something else; she not only knew how to handle it but had plenty of shells, and so far had been able to keep the outlaws at a respectable distance.

Outlaws. Once again she turned her eyes in their direction. A tightness filled her throat. Three of them were coming up the floor of the swale. Something in the way they rode told her that this time they intended to finish the job of taking over the wagons.

"All of you—keep down low back there," she warned, and twisted about to see where the cowboy's horse was standing. If there was a rifle hanging from the saddle, she wanted it.

Disappointment flowed through her. The horse, a big sorrel, was standing a half-dozen yards away. She'd never have time to reach the animal and get the rifle, if indeed there was one, and make it back into the wagon before the outlaws arrived. She would have to make the shotgun and the cowboy's pistol—if she could make it work—do.

"Sibyl—"

Thalia smiled faintly at the reassuring tone of her mother's voice. For her youngest daughter Martha Tallant seldom used the pet name, Sassy, that her husband had given the girl. "Bring me that can of black powder from the chuck box. I've got to stop this bleeding. Then I'll need that jar of Grandma Gooch's salve. He's not hurt bad."

"Is he coming to?" Sibyl asked.

"Not yet, but he will in a few minutes, I expect."

Thalia looked again to the outlaws. They were no more than a quarter mile away. She had hoped the cowboy would

have regained consciousness by then. Crouching down between the seat and the dash, she rested the barrel of the
shotgun on the edge of the wagon bed and watched the
riders draw near.

"Those outlaws are coming," she called back without
turning. "When the shooting starts, remember what I said
—stay down low."

"I can help you," Augusta said. "I've used that shotgun
before."

"Then come up here with me," Thalia said. She gave the
idea a moment's thought. "Maybe you can use the cowboy's pistol."

"I can sure try," Augusta said as she climbed over into
the seat, and crouched down beside her older sister.
"When do we start shooting?" she added, picking up the
pistol. "They're getting pretty close."

"Right now," Thalia replied, and triggered the two barrels of the shotgun in rapid order at the outlaws.

Augusta drew back the hammer of the revolver she held,
took a firm grip of the weapon with both hands. The .44
roared, adding its belch of smoke and thunderous sound to
that of the shotgun.

The outlaws slowed briefly, and then came on but with
less bravado. Reloading, Thalia watched them narrowly
through the haze. They were beginning to slant directly
toward the wagons.

"Let them get closer," she murmured, as she readied the
long-barreled gun again. "We can't hit them when they're
so far away . . . How are you doing with the cowboy's
gun?"

"All right I guess. It about jumps out of my hands when I
fire it—and I'll need some cartridges—"

"Tell Mama to hand you his gun belt—" Thalia replied,
and then broke off abruptly as the outlaws opened fire.

Bullets thudded into the side of the wagon, ripped

through the canvas top, and dug into the ground near the horses, sending up little spurts of dirt. Both teams began to shy nervously. Tight lipped, Thalia triggered the shotgun again. Nearby Augusta was having trouble with the hammer of the cowboy's pistol, but finally managed to draw it back and get off another shot.

"More outlaws!" she cried in a falling voice as she leaned back.

Thalia, engaged in reloading, glanced up. Three riders on a ridge to the east were silhouetted against the gray sky.

"You shoot at them when they start down the slope," Thalia said grimly. "I'll try to hold off the others."

Raising her weapon, she sighted down the twin barrels at the outlaws on the road. She paused. The trio had halted, their horses fiddling against tight reins. In the next bit of time the riders on the ridge headed down the grade firing their guns at the outlaws.

"They're not with the other bunch!" Augusta cried, her voice filled with relief.

"What is it? What's happening?" Martha Tallant's anxious voice called from the depths of the wagon.

"We'll have to wait and see," Thalia answered. "Some men showed up and drove off the ones that killed Papa. They may be just more outlaws set on robbing us like the others—"

"They're coming back!" Augusta cut in. "What'll we do?"

"Just have your gun ready. We won't let them get too close."

The three riders approached at a lope. Thalia waited until they were within fifty yards or so, and then triggered the left barrel of the shotgun. Dirt, mud, twigs and dead leaves spouted up in front of the riders. They pulled to an abrupt stop.

"Hello, the wagons!" one of the men called. "Hold your fire—we're lawmen!"

"Lawmen!" Martha Tallant said in deep relief. "Oh, thank God!"

"Lawmen—maybe," Thalia called back, keeping the shotgun trained on the men. "What do you want?"

"My name's Henry Guzman," the rider slightly forward of the others answered. He was a thick-set man wearing a yellow duster. "We've trailed a bank robber to this area. You see a lone man rider by?"

"Are you a sheriff?"

"I'm a railroad detective—and a deputy sheriff. Men with me are my deputies. Anybody in your party get hurt by those renegades?"

Thalia thought for a long breath. Truth was inherent within her, but the last thing she wanted, for some unknown reason, was to have lawmen poking around the wagons.

"Tell them they killed Papa and—" Augusta began, and fell silent as her older sister raised a warning hand.

Thalia shook her head. "They may be looking for the cowboy—and we need him. If we tell them about Papa they'll be over here wanting to help."

"Why should we care about him? If he—"

"Like I said we may need him. Those lawmen will ride on and the outlaws will probably come back. Anyway I think we owe him something—and he doesn't look like a criminal to me." Thalia said, and turned her attention back to Guzman and his deputies.

"We'll make out," she called. "Thanks, anyway. We're obliged to you for driving off those outlaws."

"No thanks necessary . . . You never did answer my question about seeing anybody ride past you headed north, or maybe south."

"No, nobody's gone by us," Thalia said truthfully.

"Those outlaws kept us real busy. A rider could have slipped by unnoticed, Deputy."

"That's about what happened," the detective said, looking off to the south. "I don't think those outlaws will trouble you again, but if you want—"

"Obliged to you but we'll be all right now. Thanks again for driving them away."

"Was all in the line of duty," the detective said, and, touching the brim of his hat with a forefinger, nodded to the men with him and started on up the swale. "Good luck."

ELEVEN

JOHN BUCKNER first became aware of a throbbing pain inside his head, and then of a burning sensation along his right temple. Gradually the mist clouding his eyes cleared, and the cobwebs smothering his brain disappeared. Fighting himself, he focussed his attention on a woman's voice coming from nearby.

"—Those outlaws kept us real busy. A rider could have slipped by unnoticed, Deputy."

Deputy! Was the woman speaking to Henry Guzman? Had the railroad detective and his posse caught up with him as he had feared might happen if he stopped to help the pilgrims?

The deputy's reply was not intelligible but when he had apparently finished the woman said, "Obliged to you but we'll be all right now. Thanks again for driving them away."

After that there was silence, broken finally when the woman said: "Everybody just stay where you are—don't move. Let them get on their way."

"Why, Thalia?" Buckner heard another voice say. It sounded like that of the older woman, who had been on the seat holding her dead husband. She was now crouched beside him, had been the one who pushed him back down when he tried to rise.

"We don't want them snooping around—"

"But if they're the law—"

"No doubt they are, and the man they're looking for is probably the one laying right there in the wagon. How is he?"

"He's coming to, I think. If he is the one—an outlaw—we should have turned him over to those lawmen."

"Don't you think we owe him something for helping us?" Thalia continued. "If he is, we can tell him to be on his way after he's able to ride."

"I'm all right now," Buckner said before the older woman could reply. He didn't care much for the idea of being talked about as if he weren't there—or perhaps was dead. "Who was that you were talking to?" he added as he drew himself to a sitting position.

Thalia had come about on the seat and was looking back at him. The others in the wagon were also studying him with interest.

"Said his name was Henry Guzman, or something like that. Claimed to be a detective and a deputy of some kind. He also said he was looking for an outlaw who had robbed a bank somewhere. Had two men with him."

So it *was* Guzman! Not only had the detective caught up with him but was now ahead. And if he had only two men with him, where was the rest of the posse? Buckner gave that some thought as he braced himself for the next question he was sure the women would put to him. Should he lie or tell the truth about his identity? But the question didn't come; either the women didn't care who he was or else were too polite to ask.

"We're the Tallant family," Thalia said. "You've already met my mother, and those two in the back there with her are Augusta and Sibyl, my sisters."

Buckner nodded and looked around. The bandage about his head seemed tight, and whatever medicine had been put on the wound smarted. Sibyl no doubt was the youngest of the girls, probably sixteen or seventeen. She was pretty in a doll-like way with reddish brown hair and what could be dark blue eyes. It was difficult to tell in the shadowy depths of the wagon. She was wearing a flowered gingham dress, he noted.

"We're from Georgia," Augusta said. "I'll bet you came from Texas, judging by that big hat you're wearing."

"There and a few other places," Buckner replied. "Was born in Missouri. Name's John Buckner." He paused, reached up and gingerly explored the bandaged wound on the side of his head with fingertips. "Reckon I got clipped pretty good by a bullet."

"That's exactly what happened," Martha Tallant said, and related what had taken place. "Things would have turned out much worse for us if you hadn't come along. And the same goes for those lawmen."

"What about that bunch that was jumping you? Where are they?"

Thalia looked back down the swale. "They're gone—or at least I don't see them anywhere. Could be those deputies scared them off for good."

Buckner shook his head gently. "Maybe."

"That mean you think they'll be back?"

"My guess would be yes . . . Where are you folks headed?"

"Colorado," Martha Tallant said. "We planned to meet my brother who lives up there and go into the ranching business with him . . . Now, I'm not sure we—"

Buckner glanced around the wagon again, once more taking note of the reinforcing and like precautionary measures that had been taken. There was little doubt it was well built but the team was something else. While strong, thick-necked Morgans, they would be no match for the long steep pulls that would face them in the high mountains ahead. The same applied to the horses pulling the other wagon. They would need help if they were to reach their intended goal.

"I don't know what we'll do without Papa," Thalia said. "Besides all the other things he drove this wagon because the horses have real hard mouths. Nobody but him could handle them."

"Fine animals, all of them," Buckner said. "From here it doesn't look like any of them got hurt. In fact, except for the loss of your pa I'd say you came through the attack real lucky."

None of the women made any comment. Martha Tallant moved over to the quilt-covered body of her husband, and reaching underneath, sought out his hand. Sibyl began to cry softly and Augusta lowered her head. After a few moments Thalia stirred, again looked off down the swale.

"Were you going to Colorado?" she asked without turning. There was a hopeful note in her tone.

"No, Arizona, or maybe Mexico," Buckner said. "Hadn't exactly made up my mind. From the set of your wagons you look to be traveling heavy."

"I guess we are," Thalia said, coming back around. "We're entertainers—a musical family I guess you could say. We travel around stopping in places where they have a town hall, or maybe a big saloon, and put on a show. During the war things changed a bit. We entertained the soldiers in the camps and forts."

"We were like gypsies," Martha said heavily. "We had a nice home once but like most everyone else we lost it—lost it and everything we owned—and now I've lost my husband."

"He played a violin beautifully," Sibyl said, "and Mama

accompanied him on the melodeon. Gussie and I danced, and sometimes Thalia would play her guitar."

Buckner, head now almost clear, again glanced about the wagon. The other vehicle would be as heavily loaded as this one, he reckoned. They could plan on having a hard time traveling through the mountains.

"We carry all of the musical instruments and our show dresses, as well as other clothing in my wagon," Thalia said as if reading his mind.

Like her youngest sister she had dark hair and blue eyes shadowed by full brows, but unlike Sibyl she was tall. The endless traveling that the family had done gave her skin a light, warm tan color like the slopes of butterfly lilies he'd seen growing along the trails during his wandering, and the oval shape of her face set off her natural beauty despite the man's shirt and baggy trousers she was wearing. He could not tell much else about her, sitting on the wagon seat as she was, but he suspected she had a fine, full figure.

"My brother's waiting for us up in Colorado," Martha Tallant said, her manner brightening. "His name is Alexander, Shadrack Alexander. We call him Shad for short. He knows all about ranching and went on ahead a few months ago so that everything would be ready when we got there."

"That mean he's already got a place?"

"Yes, and a very fine one according to a letter that we got from him. It's near a town called Corinth. Do you know where that is? Have you ever been there?"

Buckner nodded, glanced out beyond the teams. It appeared to be growing darker, and he guessed clouds were gathering for more rain. An uneasiness began to fill him. Another storm would mean more trouble for the Tallants —and he was far from convinced the outlaw bunch that had attacked the wagons was gone.

"Recollect being through there once, maybe twice. It's north of the Pass, near the Arkansas River."

"Will it be a good place to live?" Augusta wondered.

"Expect it will. Winters get a mite cold but other folks have managed to get through them, reckon you will, too. Only one thing—"

"What's that?" Martha Tallant asked quickly.

"It'll be a long, hard pull to the Arkansas. Your teams will never make it without help."

The women glanced at each other in dismay. "Our horses," Augusta said, "we thought we had the best. How can—"

"You'll find teamsters at Willow Springs—that's a settlement at the foot of the Pass—Raton Pass it's called. You can hire one of them to hitch onto your rigs and pull you over to the other side."

Martha Tallant sighed audibly, and then, still holding onto the hand of her dead husband, she turned her troubled eyes to Buckner. Off in the trees to the west a dove mourned softly.

"Can—can we hire you to see us over this Pass—into Colorado? I'll pay whatever you want. We don't have a lot of money, just what we were able to accumulate since the war ended, so we can't spare much."

Buckner stirred, brushed at the whiskers on his jaw. He was aware that Sibyl was staring at him intently, a hopeful look in her eyes. Again he rubbed at his jaw. He needed to go north in the same direction Guzman and his men had taken about as much as he needed a rattlesnake bite, but the women would have to have help. They'd not even make it to Willow Springs otherwise. He reckoned he could give them a hand to there, turn them over to a couple of reliable teamsters who would get them over the Pass, and then pull out—assuming he hadn't run into Henry Guzman.

"Forget paying me anything," he said, drawing himself partly erect and moving toward the front of the wagon. "I figure I owe you folks."

"Then you'll stay with us—drive Papa's team?" Thalia asked quickly.

He nodded, seeing smiles of relief come onto the faces of the women. Sibyl pushed forward impulsively and kissed him on the cheek.

"Oh, thank you," she murmured.

Surprised, Buckner hesitated, grinned. "We best move on right away. Being out in the open like this's not a good idea. Good chance that bunch of outlaws will come back . . . Won't be able to go far. Be dark soon and it's starting to rain again."

"I—we can bury my husband then," Martha said in a forlorn voice. "I hate to think of leaving him out here in this wilderness, but—"

"Only thing we can do, Mama," Thalia said, as she climbed from the wagon. Buckner, saying nothing, stepped onto the iron-tired wheel of the vehicle and dropped to the ground beside the girl.

"We'll move out soon as I tie my horse onto the back of the wagon."

Augusta had dismounted and was hurrying toward the other vehicle. Thalia started to follow, but paused. At that moment he heard Sibyl speak to her mother.

"I want to ride with you and him," she said. There was a petulant tone in her voice.

Buckner heard Martha agree indifferently, and turned to Thalia. "Something you wanted to say?"

Her lovely features were serious as she brought her attention back to him. Off in the trees the dove cooed again.

"Just want to get everything straight," she said. "We can't afford to make a mistake, and if we're about to I want to put a stop to everything right here and now."

Buckner looked more closely at her in the failing light.

She was, he thought, the best-looking woman he had ever seen—and she was worried.

"I reckon I know what's bothering you."

"I expect you do," Thalia said. "Are you the outlaw those deputies are looking for?"

TWELVE

IN THE SILENCE that followed Augusta halted and looked back. Sibyl and her mother edged closer to the seat in order to better hear his reply.

"I reckon I am," he said finally in a drawling voice. "I'm the one they're tracking—but I didn't rob that bank, I just collected what was owed me."

"Owed you?" Thalia echoed in frank disbelief.

Down the way, in the direction the outlaws had fled, a gunshot echoed flatly through the hush.

"That's right, owed me, or maybe I best say the railroad did. The money I took was from them."

"Why did the railroad owe you money?" Augusta asked, moving back to where she stood beside Thalia.

"Was a deal made for my property back in Missouri," Buckner said, and explained what it was all about. "They were supposed to pay me years ago, but never did."

Thunder rumbled off in the distance. Martha Tallant waited until it had finished and then said, "So you just went in this bank with a gun in your hand, and took the money." She shook her head. "That was robbery—you can't deny it."

"But, Mama, they owed it to him!" Sibyl exclaimed. "It was his money."

"Not necessarily," the older woman said. "They had to give it to him first before it was his. When he just went in and took it—that makes it robbery."

Buckner frowned, puzzled by Martha's logic, but said nothing. He glanced questioningly at Thalia, wondering how she felt about it. Her lips were compressed tightly as she studied him.

"We have a lot at stake here," the girl said after a time. "Our future, everything we own—"

"Actually our lives," Augusta added.

"Are in your hands," Thalia finished.

Buckner shrugged. "If you're afraid I'm going to rob you—"

Thalia nodded. "It's been in our minds. You've probably guessed that we're carrying some money, our part of what it will take to buy the ranch. We can't risk losing it."

"You won't, far as I'm concerned—and you need me to get to Colorado."

Augusta stiffened and her face hardened. Like the other Tallant women she had blue eyes, but her hair was a straw color, and gathered in a bun on the nape of her neck. Also in gingham, she was pretty and well shaped.

"We've come this far without you!" she said angrily.

"But we had Papa then," Thalia said. "Don't forget that."

Buckner pulled his hat lower over his eyes. He supposed he should tell the women that if that was how they felt, they could forget him, just head on north for the Colorado mountains without him. For his own sake it would be the smartest thing he could do—but he couldn't find it in his heart or conscience to pull out on them. He glanced up at Martha Tallant.

"You got your doubts about me, too?"

"Well, I'm not sure if—"

Buckner shook his head impatiently. "Makes no differ-

ence. You'll have me with you until we get to Willow
Springs, maybe through the Pass if we can't find any teamsters willing to take you on. I'm damned if I'll leave you on
your own! Any chance your brother will come to meet
you?"

"I doubt it. All he knows is that we're on the way. He has
no idea when we'll be getting there. By late summer was all
we ever told him."

Abruptly Buckner wheeled and crossed to where his
horse was standing. They were wasting precious time by
useless talking. Taking up the reins, he led the sorrel to the
back of the Tallant wagon and tied him securely to a tailgate eyebolt. Returning to the front of the vehicle, he
swung up to the seat. Only then did he notice that Thalia
and Augusta had not moved.

"We're moving out," he said, unwinding the reins from
the whipstock. "Aim to go as far as possible before dark."

Thalia favored him with an icy stare. "Are you going to
be giving the orders from now on?"

Buckner smiled briefly. "Count on it."

The young woman nodded. "All right, but keep this in
mind—I'll have my shotgun handy every minute. If you
make one false move I'll blow your head off!"

"Thalia!" Martha Tallant said in a shocked, reproving
voice. "There was no need for that!"

"Well, we've never had any truck with an outlaw before," Thalia said evenly. "We had all better keep an eye
on him or we're liable to lose—"

"Get in your wagon," Buckner cut in. "I'll be working
my way through the trees. Try and keep up."

"Don't worry, I know how to drive," Thalia snapped,
and with Augusta stalked off across the open ground to her
vehicle.

Buckner kicked off the brake and cut the team and
wagon left. There was no road but he did spot a trail that

bore northwest, and taking his lead from that, guided the horses along it. At times it ran through fairly open ground, at others he was forced to drive the rig in between densely growing trees where space was so narrow the wheels of the wagon tore and rubbed against their trunks. Low-growing brush was a hindrance at times, too, causing the wagon to bounce and jolt, and creak ominously, as the iron-tired wheels passed over the clumps. It was difficult, shoulder-wrenching driving, and several times Buckner looked back to reassure himself that Thalia and Augusta were all right. He need not have troubled himself; the Tallants' eldest daughter was maintaining her position a wagon's length behind.

The sky overhead was steadily darkening, both from the overcast and the lateness of the day. Buckner turned his head to speak to Martha, who, with Sibyl, had elected to remain in the back of the vehicle.

"Best we pull up pretty soon," he said. "We'll make camp for the night. Horses look like they could use some rest—and feed."

"There's a sack of grain in the other wagon," the woman said.

"Fine. Expect all of you could use a good meal, too."

"I sure could!" Sibyl said, leaning against the back of the seat. "I'm hungry."

"We've been on the run all day—ever since those out-laws started after us. Have you had anything today?"

"Not since morning—or maybe it was last night," he replied. "Feeling a little gaunt myself."

Martha Tallant's hostility seemed to have cooled. "We don't have much—we were hoping to come to a mercantile where we could stock up—but I think the girls and I can get something together," she said as she climbed up onto the seat beside him.

"Will it still be light enough for me to bury my husband?" she asked as the wagon topped a slight rise and started down the opposite side.

Buckner nodded. "I'll see to it—"

"I don't know if I'll ever get over him being gone," Martha murmured.

Buckner shrugged. "Someone once told me that you don't ever get over the death of a loved one—that you just learn to live with it. I believe that."

"I guess it's true," Martha said, and twisted around to comfort Sibyl, who had begun to cry again.

Buckner looked back once more. Thalia and her wagon were close behind. He brought his attention again to the faint trail they were following. Ahead he saw a break in the trees and underbrush. Along its far side was the dull glint of water.

"We can make camp along that creek," he said, pointing.

He heard Martha Tallant sigh deeply and guessed she welcomed his words. The long, frightful day, the rough jostling of the wagon as they moved up the mountainside no doubt had brought all of the women to near exhaustion.

A short time later Buckner drew to a halt on the opposite bank of the stream, a small, muddy affair no more than an arm's length in width. It would not be an ideal camp as the ground was uneven and the water would have to be strained for their use, but he felt it was best for all to stop.

Thalia pulled up close by, following his direction, and both she and Augusta, stiff and as distant as before, climbed down from the wagon. He gave them both a short grin and said, "We'll unhitch the teams but leave the harness on. Can slip the bridles if you like. Make it easier for them to eat."

Thalia made no reply but immediately began to unhook the traces and release the wagon tongue. When the horses were free she didn't wait for Buckner to speak but led the

pair off to a stand of grass nearby. Buckner, his team un-
hitched, followed with it.

"I don't figure we'll need to hobble them," he said, slipping the bridles. "With all that leather hanging on them, I
don't think they'll wander off."

Thalia still made no comment but began to remove the
bridles from her horses.

"Expect we ought to give them a bite of the grain you've
got in your wagon. I'll go get—"

Thalia nodded curtly. "Don't bother. I'll take care of it."

Buckner studied her for several moments, and then
shrugged and walked back to where Martha and her two
other daughters were setting up camp. That they had done
so often was evident as each appeared to have certain, spe-
cific chores to perform, all of which they were going about
accomplishing in a businesslike manner.

"Is it all right to build a fire?" the older woman asked
when she saw him approaching.

He nodded. "Keep it small. I'll rustle you up some dry
wood."

"No, let Sibyl do it. That has been her job."

Buckner glanced at the youngest sister. "Do you know
where to find dry wood?"

"Of course!" Sibyl said with a wide smile. "I find it under the trees and bushes, and there are always dead limbs
and branches in the trees that haven't got soaked."

Buckner smiled and turned to Augusta, who had made a
faint derisive sound. It was evident what her thoughts were,
that she and her sisters and mother were no babes in the
woods, and could very well make it to Colorado without his
help if there hadn't been a driver problem and there were
no outlaws to contend with.

Taking the spade he saw affixed to the side of one of the
wagons, he moved off to a slight hill to their left, and there
spent the next half hour digging a grave in the soft, water-

soaked ground. He had just finished when Sibyl came to summon him to supper. Laying the spade aside, he paused at the stream to wash his hands in the silted water, and then joined the women gathered about the low fire.

It was an excellent meal by his standards, which were based upon his own efforts on the trail, and he enjoyed the strong coffee, fried meat, potatoes savored with onions, gravy and warmed bread to the fullest. When he was finished he rose, smiled and inclined his head slightly to the women.

"I've never had a better meal in my life—not even in some of the fancy restaurants I've been to."

"Thank you, Mr. Buckner," Martha Tallant said, returning his smile. "Maybe you were just hungry."

Thalia flung an angry look of disapproval at her mother, expressing dislike for her parent's display of friendliness. Buckner, noting it in the faint light, grinned, and shook his head.

"Expect I'd best double back a ways and see if there are any signs of those outlaws." He paused, reading the thought, *you can keep on going far as I'm concerned,* on Thalia's face. "Ought to be back in about an hour. I'll help with the burying then."

"Take care!" Sibyl called sweetly as he turned to his horse.

"Just what I aim to do," he replied with a grin, and pulling his rifle from the saddle boot, handed it to Augusta. "You might need this while I'm gone. Expect you know how to use it."

Augusta shrugged. "You cock this thing called the hammer, look down the barrel and then you pull what's called the trigger," the light-haired Tallant daughter replied dryly. "Yes, I know how."

"Good enough," Buckner said, irritated by the women's attitude. He could do without their sarcasm and hostility, he thought as he mounted the sorrel and swung away, but he knew he had no choice except to put up with it until he got them to Raton Pass. Once there he just might let them shift for themselves.

THIRTEEN

AWAY FROM THE GLARE of the fire, in the near full dark, Buckner found it easy to follow the tracks of the wagons. The prints left by their wheels in the rain-softened ground were deep set and he had no difficulty in retracing the route they had taken earlier. Nor would Henry Guzman or the outlaws, he thought grimly.

The sorrel, benefitting from the feed and water and good if brief rest, was now in a lively condition, and they quickly reached the edge of the trees. There Buckner halted for a time, and, certain there was no one in the immediate vicinity, rode out into the open where he would have a view of the country both to the north and the south.

The sun was gone, having dropped behind a heavy embankment of clouds at least an hour ago, and vision was limited, but he studied the swale long and carefully. There were no apparent signs of either the outlaws or the detective and his posse anywhere.

Guzman, he decided, could be forgotten for the time being. Logically he would have continued on toward Colorado and points beyond, and would not stop until finally convinced he'd taken a wrong trail. The outlaws were an entirely different matter.

He had said little about it to the Tallants but he was sure

they would show up again. Four women, thought to be alone since it looked as if the men with them had both been cut down, would be easy pickings. And they'd have no fear of the lawmen who had driven them off; they would have watched and satisfied themselves that the three riders had continued on north.

Not only was it reasonable to think the outlaws would try again but John Buckner had a deep-seated feeling that they'd be back, a real hunch, and such before had never failed him. The best thing he could do was let the Tallant horses rest for the night, and figure to move out well before daylight in the morning. He supposed there would be opposition to it, but he would have to ignore any protests; regardless of what anyone thought, the threat of danger was there.

He could see no indications of a camp anywhere to the south—the faint glow of a fire in the darkness above the trees or out on the flat; but that meant little as they could have passed up building a fire or kept it low and thoroughly shielded to where it threw no light. Nevertheless, Buckner was certain the outlaws were still around, visible or not. After an hour's time, he turned the sorrel about and headed back for the camp along the creek.

Drawing near, he intentionally swung off the dual tracks left by the wagons. The women were a mite hard to convince, and he wanted to impress upon them the ever present danger they all faced. Shortly the moon broke out of the overcast, and now, slipping in and out of the clouds periodically, brightened the hushed grove for a short time and then plunged it back again into darkness. No night birds could be heard, the only sound being the shrill barking of coyotes somewhere in the higher hills.

He circled completely around and came up to the wagons from the west. The women were gathered around the low fire, and the first thing he heard was the mentioning of his name.

"Said his name was John Buckner." It was Thalia's voice. "Maybe that's true and maybe it's just a name he's made up."

"Why would he do that?" Martha wondered.

"Men running from the law always change their names," Thalia explained. "They have to if they hope to escape."

Regret flowed through Buckner. He was sorry Thalia felt as she did about him. He liked her looks and the way she handled herself—which all boiled down in his mind to her being beautiful as well as capable.

"Well, I like him and I don't believe he's an outlaw!" Sibyl's voice was high and held a note of defiance. "And I think he's fine and handsome!"

"Oh, Sassy, you'd think the devil was fine and handsome if he showed up in a new suit!" Augusta said. "And don't go getting ideas about him. You know our agreement—Thalia marries first, and then me. You come last."

"I don't care what—" Sibyl began when her mother's reproachful words cut her off.

"Now, girls—never mind! I'm grateful to God that he came along when he did. With your papa dead we need a man."

"But an outlaw?" Thalia said, questioningly.

There was a silence and then the older woman said quietly, "Outlaw or not—do we have a choice? He insists on helping us, and we all know we need help. We have only a vague idea of where we are or where the next town is. Too, those outlaws are around close, somewhere."

"I think Buckner feels he owes us something for hiding him from those lawmen," Augusta said. "It could be his intentions are good."

"Well, they better be!" Thalia declared firmly. "Otherwise he's going to get a dose of bird shot."

"Never mind that kind of talk," Martha Tallant said. "We'll all keep an eye on him, and as long as he's honest with us, we'll be honest with him. We've got to remember that old saying about never looking a gift horse in the mouth."

Buckner, feeling a bit guilty at eavesdropping, rode out of the darkness into the glow of the fire. Immediately all conversation ceased and remained so while he dismounted, loosened the sorrel's cinch and removed the bridle preparatory to staking out the big sorrel where he could graze and get to water.

"Did you see them?" Martha asked, filling a tin cup with coffee from the pot nestling in the coals, and handing it to him.

"No, but they're out there," he said with a wave toward the south. "And they could have found it mighty easy to slip up on you while you were sitting here gabbing. You should have had sentries out—one at each end of the camp. You never heard me come in at all."

"That mean you were out there in the dark listening to us?" Thalia demanded angrily.

Nodding, he took a swallow of coffee. "Wanted you to realize that you're in country where you can't take chances like you did."

Thalia's features were tight set. "I suppose you got your ears full of what we were saying."

Buckner grinned. "Yes'm, I sure did," he drawled. "Some of it I appreciated, the rest I don't give a damn about."

In the quiet that followed, Sibyl leaned forward and tossed a handful of dry branches on the dwindling fire. An owl hooted in the distance, breaking the hush of the moon and starlit dappled night. Buckner downed the last of his coffee.

"Expect we'd best take care of your husband," he said to

Martha. "We had a gray sunset. Means more rain, and we've got to move out early."

"We've already buried my husband. The girls and I took care of that while you were gone."

Buckner's respect for the four women mounted another notch. "Sorry I wasn't here to help, but I felt I'd better see—"

"We managed," Thalia said stiffly. "How far are we from the next town—the one at the foot of the Pass?"

"Seventy-five, maybe a hundred miles. Can't be sure."

"Means five or six days traveling—"

"If we were in flat, open country, yes. Through the mountains it'll take longer."

"Longer," Sibyl murmured in a falling voice. "I was hoping we'd soon come to civilization where we could—"

"Never mind," Martha said. "We'll eventually get there, and till then we'll just have to make the best of it."

"What's the name of the town?" Augusta asked.

"Willow Springs. It's at the foot of the Pass. Some folks call it Raton. Think I mentioned this earlier," he continued after a time, "but we'd best make an early start in the morning, and you all need to get some rest. However, there's something else we'll have to do—post guards. I'll take the first three hours."

"No," Martha cut in. "You've had a long, hard day, you even got hurt. I want you to get some sleep. We'll take care of standing watch."

Buckner rubbed at his jaw. "I'm not sure that's a good idea. Those outlaws—"

"Don't fret about it!" Thalia snapped. "We can do something as simple as that as well as you—Gussie, you and Sibyl can start off. Go down the trail—"

Buckner shrugged. "Go to where that rock-faced bluff—we came right by it. You can follow the wagon tracks. It'll be a good place to watch from. You can see riders coming for a couple of hundred yards if the moon will stay out."

"What'll we do if we see them?" Augusta asked. "There's at least three of them, maybe more, and there'll be only one of us with a gun—if I'm to carry that," she added, pointing to his rifle propped against a nearby tree.

"Just don't try doing anything. Soon as you spot them coming come back to camp and let me know."

"How far is that rocky place from here?" Martha asked.

"Hundred yards more or less."

The older woman nodded in satisfaction. "That'll give the girls plenty of time to warn us. Now, you climb into the wagon and get some sleep. Thalia and I will spell off Sibyl and Augusta in three hours. After that you can take over."

Buckner smiled. He needed no urging to catch a few winks of sleep, and the women, with the exception of Thalia, could sleep tomorrow while they were traveling. He rose and moved toward the wagon. Thalia also came to her feet, shotgun cradled in her arms. As she faced him he could sense the hostility that still filled her.

"Do you really think we're in danger from those outlaws?" she asked. Her features were serious, and her eyes, shadowed by the low fire, were barely visible. "After those lawmen drove them off I'd think they'd be afraid to try anything."

"Meant nothing to them. Soon as that deputy and his men were out of sight they started making plans."

"That's only a guess—"

Buckner shrugged indifferently. "Whatever you say, but we're going to keep our guard up all night, and every day and night after this until we've reached Willow Springs."

Thalia's expression did not change. Murmuring something unintelligible, she turned and walked to her wagon, climbed aboard where she joined her mother. Augusta and

Sibyl had moved off and were already on the trail to where they would assume sentry positions.

Buckner would have preferred to stand the first watch himself, and the entire night, but Martha Tallant had insisted on a different arrangement, and he was too beat to protest. Swinging up into the other wagon, which appeared to be more roomy, he stretched out on the pallet that had been laid for him and was quickly asleep.

He had scarcely closed his eyes, it seemed, when he felt someone shaking his shoulder, and sat up immediately.

"What is it?"

Martha Tallant was bending over him. "Something terrible has happened!" she answered in a trembling voice. "Those outlaws came back—and they've kidnapped Sibyl!"

FOURTEEN

BUCKNER WAS UP and out of the wagon in a single move. A lantern had been lit and hung from the side of the vehicle and in its glow he could see Thalia and Augusta standing nearby. Augusta was weeping hysterically but the oldest sister was silent, her features grim. As Martha joined them, she too began to cry. Anger was burning through Buckner.

"What the hell happened?" he demanded, crossing hurriedly to his horse.

"Gussie says they were at the rocky place where you told them to watch," Thalia replied, "and—"

"We heard a noise down the trail a little ways—only a little ways," Augusta explained, managing to control her sob. "Sassy thought we should see what it was—that maybe it was the outlaws coming."

Buckner had slipped the sorrel's bridle back into place, was now pulling tight the cinch.

"Oh, I should have never let her go alone!" Augusta cried. "I should have—"

"You should have both come back here and told me," Buckner snapped.

"We thought that if it was them we'd have more time to get back here and get you," Augusta said. "But we weren't sure about anything—about whether it was them or maybe just some animal. I guess now it was the outlaws."

"I guess it was," Buckner said.

"Sassy didn't come back," Augusta continued, sobs again breaking her voice. "I waited a few minutes and then went to find her. There wasn't a sign, but I think I heard horses running somewhere out there in the swale."

The sorrel ready, Buckner turned to the women. "Want you all to stay close—stay in the wagon until I get back."

"I'm going with you," Thalia said. "There's at least three of them, maybe more. You'll need help."

"Most help you can give me is do what I said," Buckner replied. "When I come back I'll sing out. I don't want you unloading that blasted scatter-gun in me."

"Isn't there something we can do?" Martha Tallant asked brokenly. "I'm—I'm so worried about Sibyl! She's so young—little more than a baby—"

An opening in the thick clouds overhead allowed the moon to reappear suddenly, and the area became bathed in a soft, silvery light. The older woman's features were tear-streaked and strained.

"Sassy's no baby, Mama," Thalia said, putting her arms about her mother. "She'll be all right."

"If I could only think—believe that, I—"

"One thing you can do," Buckner interrupted, "is hitch up the teams and be ready to pull out." He looked more closely at the older woman, smiled, and in a kind voice added, "Don't worry, I'll bring her back."

At once he swung up into the saddle, and circling the wagons, rode onto the trail. The best place to start looking for the girl, he reasoned, was where the two sisters had set up their watch. Too, Augusta had said she'd heard horses out on the flat of the swale; that would mean the outlaws, if they were the ones who had taken Sibyl, had struck off to the south. Such could be proof that it was the same outlaws who had killed Tallant and tried to take over the wagons when he'd come onto the scene. But why? Was it the women they wanted, or was there something else?

Buckner was considering that question when he reached the rocks. He halted there, listening and thinking. One thing was certain—he'd have to find Sibyl quickly. A young, pretty girl in the hands of several hard-case outlaws would be in for a time of horror. After a bit he rode on until he reached the point where the wagons had entered the grove. Turning onto the flat, he again halted, and standing in his stirrups, searched the country to the south for a sign of the outlaw camp.

Rain was beginning to fall again, this time in large, scattered drops. Ignoring it, Buckner continued to scan the dark band of trees extending southward, hoping to see a fire glow somewhere in the thickening gloom. He didn't think the outlaws would be too far away, and he doubted taking the girl for their own pleasure was all they had in mind. But what other reason could they have?

Buckner started the sorrel, walking slowly, along the edge of the grove. He kept in the shadows as much as possible although the rain-filled darkness was more than sufficient to mask his presence. The moon was hidden behind a mass of clouds again and there were no intermittent surges of light as there had been earlier. The shower ceased for a brief time and then began again.

Far to the northwest lightning split the sky and thunder rolled ominously. A heavy storm was raging in that part of the mountains, he reckoned, and hoped that it would stay well to the west and not present problems for him and the Tallant women when they moved on to Willow Springs.

Abruptly he drew the sorrel to a stop. Not too far ahead, a short distance to the right in the grove, he caught the faint glow of a fire. It was very faint and at first he was uncertain whether his eyes were tricking him or not, but cutting back into the trees, moving carefully and quietly with the rain pattering down upon his hunched figure constantly, he approached the pale glare. As he drew nearer he became convinced it was a campfire. Evidently the outlaws —if the camp was theirs—did not believe anyone would be looking for them on such a dark, wet night.

Buckner pressed on slowly, his hopes rising. He gave no thought to the outlaws having any of their party out as sentries; they would consider themselves safe until morning when they could expect a search party, consisting of the three remaining women, to come looking for the missing member of the family. He doubted they would expect him to be with them, as they had seen him go down when the glancing bullet had struck him in the head. And since they had seen no more of him after that, they would assume that both he and the man who had been driving one of the wagons were dead.

If true, all well and good; it would give him an edge, something he'd need if he was to rescue Sassy Tallant. He could only hope the girl would not divulge the fact that he was still alive. Again he drew the sorrel to a halt. He had heard the sound of voices and caught the heavy smell of smoke. The glare had strengthened, all of which could mean only that the camp was close-by.

Dismounting, Buckner let his hand drop to the weapon on his hip to assure himself of its presence, and then, leading the horse, he advanced slowly toward the sound of the voices and the glow. Drawing close, he stopped, wrapped the sorrel's reins about a clump of oak, and then, .44 in hand, ducked low and moved in on the camp.

Three men—three horses. Evidently they had buried the member who had been killed in the attack on the wagons. A tarp had been strung between four pine trees, forming a canopy that sheltered them from the persistent rain. Two men, facing the low fire, were sitting just within its spread.

Raising himself slightly, Buckner searched about through the misty night for Sibyl Tallant. He located her a short distance beyond the canopy, sitting with ankles and hands bound, a slicker draped over her head and shoulders, back to a large pine. Crouched before her was one of the outlaws—the young one Buckner had noticed during the attack. He appeared to be talking to the girl, who was smiling faintly.

Buckner studied the situation. He would have to make a move that in no way would endanger the girl. With the two older outlaws to his left, separated by a dozen feet or so from the younger man, or boy, he would be at a big disadvantage. If the boy, speaking to Sibyl, who thankfully appeared to be unharmed so far, would rejoin his partners, freeing the girl would not pose such a problem.

But it looked as if the outlaw had no intention of leaving Sassy Tallant's company; indeed, she seemed to be enjoying the attention. Buckner drew back deeper into the wet, scrubby growth that ringed the small clearing in which the camp lay. He would have to come at the outlaws from a different angle, one in which the girl would not be in the line of fire.

Leaving the sorrel picketed to the oak brush, Buckner circled the camp, coming to a halt when he reached a point almost directly opposite to where he had been. Sibyl was now out of his line of fire as well as that of the outlaws, and he was in a position to cover the three men with no problem. All he need do—

"Hello—the camp!"

The hail came from the depths of the grove beyond the camp. The two older outlaws came to their feet. The one engaged in talking to Sibyl also rose, and stood facing the direction of the call.

"It's me—Nate! Don't shoot!"

"Bateman," one of the men said, shoulders going down

as his hand fell away from the gun at his side. "Damn you, Nate, it's a good thing you sung out. I'd a-plugged you sure!"

A horse and rider appeared at the edge of the firelight flare, the animal walking gingerly as if afraid of the flickering flames. The rider, a heavy-set man in what looked to be old Union army clothing, mopped at the rainwater on his bearded face as, slumped in the saddle, he pulled to a halt.

"You got a drink handy?" he asked as he swung down from a scarred old McClellan. "Been one hell of a week. Rained all the way from the Animas."

Nate Bateman. The name sounded familiar to Buckner as he crouched low in the brush, but he could not exactly place the man.

"Sure, Nate, got a quart—or what's left of one—right here," the outlaw nearest the fire said, and handed a bottle to the newcomer. "You know anything special?"

"Nope," Bateman replied, glancing about. "Where's Lobo?"

"Dead. Got put under when we was trying to stop them wagons. Sure made them folks pay for it, though! We cut down the jasper that was driving one of the wagons and some cowhand that horned in on the shooting."

Bateman took a long swallow from the bottle and let his gaze settle on Sibyl Tallant. "Who the hell's that?"

"One of the women from the wagons. Aim to hang onto her. Can use her for trading—like a ransom. Just might save us some shooting."

"She'll come in right handy for something else, too," Bateman said, grinning broadly.

FIFTEEN

THE BOY with Sibyl stiffened. "You leave her alone, hear me? She ain't much more than a kid."

Bateman tipped the bottle to his lips and treated himself to another drink. He was wet to the skin despite the slicker he was wearing, and water dripped steadily off him.

"You ain't no more'n a kid yourself," he said, "and you best watch your tongue. Just who the hell are you?"

One of the other outlaws waved a deprecating hand at Bateman. "Keep your shirt on, Nate, he's my boy . . . Come on over here, Ben, and shake hands with Nate Bateman."

Ben crossed slowly under the canopy and took the outlaw's extended hand. The fire blazed up as the vaquero tossed a handful of dry wood into the flames.

"Expect you known Chino Anaya," the older outlaw continued.

"Yeh, we've done met," Bateman said, ignoring the Mexican. "Sure do hate to hear that about old Lobo. Was a good one to ride the ridges with."

"Well, it cuts down the split," the older man said, shrugging.

"That it sure does, Pete."

The older man drew out a blackened briar pipe, glanced

at its bowl, and then taking a small firebrand from the fire, puffed its half-smoke contents into life.

"What about up north, Nate? You get the money out of that four-flusher, Alexander?"

"About a thousand dollars," Bateman replied. "It's all he had on him when he up and croaked on me."

Alexander! The name struck a chord in Buckner's mind. Alexander was the brother of Martha Tallant, the man with whom they planned to go in partnership.

"That ain't much," Pete said, putting the pipe back in his pocket and reclaiming the bottle of whiskey. He sat back down on the folded blanket he had been occupying.

"Well, was all he had," Bateman shot back angrily. "If you're hinting that I maybe—"

"Ain't hinting nothing, Nate—you know that. Just ain't as much as we was hoping for."

"No, I reckon it ain't," Bateman said, mollified. "What about this bunch he was joining up with? You for certain they're still around?"

"We've got one of the women, ain't we? That guarantees they'll stay around. And there ain't but them—three women. The man that was with them's dead. Got put under when we tried to hold them up—same as the cowboy. Alexander say how much cash they're carrying?"

"Five or six thousand. When are you figuring on us getting it?"

"In the morning. Be easy. Just have to ride up there and—"

"Ride where?"

"Couple of miles north. Camped there, and like we said, ain't nobody we have to deal with but some women, four all together counting the young one there. Way I figure it, we won't have no trouble making a deal when the old woman sees the hole card we're holding."

The outlaws had gathered into a group under the tarp,

out of the rain's reach. John Buckner edged forward, close to Sibyl. Watching the outlaws carefully, he picked up a small pebble and tossed it at the girl. It struck her on the arm. Immediately she turned and looked his way.

Pressing a finger to his lips, Buckner dropped to his belly, and again cast a look at the outlaws. They were still occupied in making their plans or discussing some other topic of importance to them. Drawing his knife, Buckner wormed his way to where the girl sat, back to the pine tree.

She watched him approach, eyes wide and filled with fear. Every few moments she flung a glance at the outlaws as if expecting one of them to turn, see Buckner, and prevent his freeing her. The same thought was coursing through Buckner's mind, also. But he was flat on the rain-soaked ground, ignoring the mud and wet grass that were plastering his clothing, while taking advantage of every clump of weeds and mound of rock and dirt that lay between him and the outlaws.

He froze. The boy, Ben, had half turned and was looking at the girl. If he decided to return to where Sibyl lay bound at the foot of the pine, Buckner realized he would have no choice but to use his gun. For a long breath Ben stared at the girl, and then when his father said something he swung his attention back to the older men.

Immediately Buckner continued working his way forward until he reached the tree where the girl was bound. Keeping the pine between himself and the outlaws, he lay up against the trunk, and extending his arms, cut the rawhide the outlaws had used to bind the girl's hands and ankles. That done, he laid a hand on her shoulder to keep her motionless until he was certain the outlaws were still occupied, and then, again warning her to be quiet, motioned for her to follow him. Sibyl reacted instantly. Getting down on the wet ground, she followed him to the brushy cover at the edge of the clearing.

Breathless, they reached it and, keeping well hidden, came to their feet. The girl started to express her thanks, but he shook his head quickly to silence her.

"Not now," he murmured. "Got to get out of here fast. My horse is over there in the trees. We'll have to—"

A yell had gone up in the camp. It was the voice of Ben. He had noticed Sibyl was missing.

"Run!" Buckner whispered urgently. "Keep low and don't make any noise."

At once he struck off through the dripping brush and trees with the girl close beside him. Over in the clearing they could hear the outlaws shouting and crashing about in the brush.

"Spread out!" someone yelled. "She sure'n hell couldn't have got far!"

Buckner slowed, veered in closer to the girl. They had rounded the west end of the clearing and were now on its north side.

"My horse—he'll be over there in a stand of trees. Get him," Buckner said, pointing.

"Where'll you be? You're not going to leave me—"

"Just start off that way—north. Go straight on. I'll catch up."

"Over here! Over here! I see them!" The voice of one of the outlaws cut through the steadily falling rain.

Buckner took the hesitant girl by the shoulders and turned her to where she faced into the direction of the sorrel.

"No time to lose!" he said in an urgent whisper, and gave her a slight shove.

"But you—what if—"

"I'll find you," he snapped and, drawing his gun, came about.

Buckner doubted the words of the man who had sung

out; likely he saw only shadows—clumps of brush and tall bushes moved by the early morning wind.

Keeping low, he ran slowly toward the clearing. He had to stop any pursuit, allow time for Sibyl and himself to get away. The outlaws were still milling about, mostly on the south side of the camp. Apparently they were convinced the girl could be found in that area. He reached the edge of the clearing and drew to an abrupt stop as one of the outlaws—the vaquero—was suddenly before him.

"*Aquí! Aquí!*" the Mexican yelled, and whipped out his gun.

Buckner drove a bullet into the crouched, vague shape of the man. He saw the vaquero stagger back and fall. At once he swung his attention to the far side of the canvas canopy. Pete, his son Ben, and the new arrival, Nate Bateman, were breaking out of the brush and starting across toward him.

Buckner, partly concealed by thick, wet foliage, triggered a quick shot at the nearest of the outlaws. All three halted, threw themselves to one side, fearing another shot and uncertain where it would be coming from. Reloading hurriedly, Buckner moved a dozen paces to his left. He fired again. The bullet drove into the soggy ground at the boots of the nearest outlaw—Bateman, sending up a spurt of mud and rain-drenched grass. Nate yelled and drew back. He slipped on the wet footing and went down hard.

There was no sign of either Ben or Pete. They had lost no time in disappearing as Bateman went down. Nor did Buckner spend a moment looking for them. He wheeled, and again keeping low, set out north, eyes switching back and forth as he searched for Sibyl and the sorrel in the thick gloom.

He caught sight of them shortly thereafter. The girl had not hurried, was intentionally keeping at a slow walk, waiting for him, he realized. Drawing abreast, he swung up into the wet saddle, and leaning down grasped Sibyl by the arm and lifted her up to a seat behind him. He could hear nothing in the direction of the outlaw camp, but he suspected they had found the body of the vaquero by then. No doubt they would immediately intensify their search for him, and failing there would undoubtedly come looking for him at the Tallant wagons.

Putting the sorrel to a lope, Buckner wound his way as fast as possible through the wet darkness until he reached the vehicles. The three women, a lantern hanging from the center bow of the wagon, were huddled in the near one. As he swung in close Thalia leaned out from beneath the canvas arch.

"Did—did you find—" she began, and then hushed as she saw her younger sister sitting behind him on the sorrel.

A sob of relief came from Martha, appearing beside Thalia. She reached out her arms as Sibyl dropped from her place on the horse and started to climb up into the wagon. Just as quickly Buckner was out of the saddle and leading the horse to the rear of the vehicle where he secured the sorrel to the tailgate.

"No time to waste!" he said in a taut voice, barely audible above the steady drumming of the rain. He glanced about. The women had broken camp and hitched up the teams as he had directed.

"I figure those outlaws will be coming this way. Can only hope the rain will wash out our tracks," he shouted, and climbing hurriedly up into the wagon, gathered the wet lines in his hands.

Martha Tallant was only a few steps behind him, as was Sibyl. When the older woman had settled beside him on the seat and the girl was safely inside the wagon, he threw a glance at the other vehicle. Through the gloom and descending rain he saw Thalia raise her hand signifying that she was ready.

At once Buckner released the brake, and slapping the team smartly on their rumps with the reins, sent the wagon lurching forward into the dark, wet night.

SIXTEEN

FOR A QUARTER MILE they drove steadily into the grove, the wagons slipping and sliding over the treacherous ground. Buckner swore under his breath at the slow pace they were being forced to maintain, but it was the best he could expect under the conditions.

The rain continued to hammer away at them, and in only minutes he and Martha Tallant, on the seat beside him, were soaked to the skin again.

"Best you get in the back," he said, as the wagon tipped dangerously to one side. "Just keep getting wetter up here."

Martha immediately crawled over the seat to where Sibyl was huddled. Taking a blanket, she handed it to Buckner.

"Drape this over yourself. It'll help a little."

He accepted the woolen cover, placed it about his shoulders and drew it about his body. It might help a little, he thought, but the constant moving of his arms as he struggled to keep the team in line would make it all but useless.

"Obliged to you," he said over a shoulder.

If the woman answered he did not hear. He was straining to look ahead, to try and avoid the washes and low slopes that threatened to overturn the wagon. Visibility was limited to only a few yards beyond the bobbing heads of the horses, and Buckner, unfamiliar as he was with the country, endeavored to see what they would be up against next.

There were no signs of the outlaws following them but he knew they could be expected to show before too long. Men on horseback would cover ground, however uncertain, much faster than wagons. He wondered too, as the lines seesawed back and forth in his hands, about Henry Guzman and his posse. Could they have heard the gunshots, and believing he had something to do with it, turned back?

It was a possibility. The detective, having failed to find him ahead, might reverse the direction of his search. If so he could expect to run headlong into the posse most anytime. All he could do was increase his vigilance.

He could hear Sibyl—somehow he found it hard to think of her as Sassy although the name more aptly fit—telling her mother of her experience in the hands of the outlaws.

"That one man—the one who came in later—said that Uncle Shad was dead—that he died on him was the way he put it. And he robbed him—"

"Did they hurt you?" Martha Tallant's question was almost blocked out by the storm.

"No," the girl replied. "One of them was young—about my age. He was nice—sort of looked after me."

"What do they want of us—did they say?"

"Our money. They talked about how much—" The girl's voice broke off abruptly as a vivid flash of lightning, followed almost immediately by a crack of thunder, split the night.

The storm was moving closer, Buckner realized. Earlier the lightning and thunder had been well to the north. Now it was evident that the worst of the storm was yet to come. John brushed at the water lashing at his face and clouding his eyes. They were in bad country for heavy rain; with the many washes and deep arroyos they could find themselves facing wild runoffs of constantly rising water building in the north and accumulating loose brush, uprooted stumps, rocks, trees and whatever else lay in its path as it roared down the mountainsides with ever-increasing force.

Leaning out from under the canvas arch, he glanced back. Through the gray veil of rain he could see the second wagon, rocking and jolting close behind. So far they had all been fortunate; neither of the wagons had gotten into trouble, and the laboring horses were holding their own on the slippery footing. Buckner straightened up, straining to see the ground ahead. Martha Tallant noted the change in his wide-shouldered frame.

"What is it? What's wrong?" she asked, leaning over the back of the seat.

"Looks like a road ahead—leastwise I can see wagon tracks."

It proved to be fairly well used, and Buckner, grateful for the break, swung the wagon onto it at once. Again he glanced back. Thalia was just turning onto the roadway and lining up on the rutted tracks left by previous pilgrims.

Traveling became easier and somewhat faster, but there was no letup in the storm. Rain continued to come down in almost impenetrable sheets while the lightning and thunder to the north increased. Smaller washes and arroyos were now running full, Buckner noticed, all of which crossed the road they were following. That set up a strong worry within him; well acquainted with the hazards of traveling through hill and mountain country during one of the fierce thunderstorms that struck periodically, he was aware of the danger.

The wagon lurched drunkenly as the right wheel dropped into a hole cut into the road by the rushing water. It came with such force and suddenness that both Martha and Sibyl screamed. Buckner, pressing himself hard against the seat, wet hands clenching the water-slicked leather reins, struggled to bring the wagon back on even keel.

Lightning continued to rip the black night, and thunder was now constant. The flashes of bluish light turned the trees and rocks around them into an eerie world that seemed intent on bringing their journey to a disastrous end.

"Can't—can't we stop?" Martha yelled. Her voice was scarcely audible above the noise of the storm and the rattling of the wagon. "I'm afraid for Thalia and Augusta—"

"We're on a downgrade," Buckner replied as the horses swerved hard left to avoid a downed tree suddenly blocking the road. "Got to find some high ground!"

He paused, turned, looked back. Despite rain slashing at his eyes, all but blinding him, he made out the dim shape of the wagon behind. Aided by the flashes of lightning, he saw Thalia, tense and hunched forward, holding tight to her team. On the opposite side of the seat, clutching the wooden bow that supported the canvas top of the wagon with one hand, the arm of the seat with the other, was Augusta. In the weird light their faces looked strained and frightened.

Abruptly the front wheels of his wagon hit solidly. The horses seemed to spring ahead as the wagon snapped, and then leveled out.

"Bottom of the slope!" he yelled as the startled women behind him cried out again. "Ought to be easier going if we're on a flat."

But it was not. Moments later Buckner became aware of their true situation. They had entered a wide arroyo. Knee-deep water carrying small branches, bushes, rocks and other debris was slashing with great force at the legs of the horses and wheels of the wagon.

"Got to get out of here!" he shouted, using the whip on

the team, and as the wagon lurched and tipped dangerously, added, "Hang on! We may go over!"

"What—what is it?" Sibyl yelled as the vehicle began to
move forward through the torrent. "I can hear—"

"You hear a flood coming down the arroyo," he said in a
taut voice as he tried to manage the horses.

"A flood? I don't understand. It's raining but—"

"Just it. Been raining all day in the higher mountains.
Builds up in the washes and canyons, then breaks loose and
comes rushing down to lower ground, bringing everything
with it."

"Oh God! Poor Thalia and Gussie! I—"

"We'll all be fine if we can cross this arroyo before it
reaches here. Brace yourself—it'll be rough going!"

A roaring sound began to fill the night. Larger shrubs
and young pines and firs came into view, bobbing and tum-
bling in the thick, muddy water. The wagon shuddered as a
large stump thudded into its side, rocking it badly as it half
floated, half skidded to the left. But the change released the
stump, and it swept on collecting brush and debris as it
raced away.

Abruptly the horses reached solid ground on the west
side of the big wash. The wagon careened wildly when the
front wheels struck the edge of the embankment. It righted
itself as the team frantically plunged on up the slight grade
with the sorrel alongside jerking at his lead rope.

"Thalia—Augusta!" Martha screamed. "Where—"

Buckner's thoughts were ahead of her words and fears.
With the wagon on safe, secure ground, he pulled the
heaving team to a halt and jammed on the brake. Thalia
would never be able to cross the raging arroyo safely, that
was certain. He leapt from the wagon and ran back to the
edge of the arroyo.

The wagon was halfway across but in trouble. The rushing water had risen and now fair-sized trees, large clumps

of brush, stumps and lesser debris were whirling about in the surging, dark water.

Unhesitating, Buckner plunged into the waist-deep torrent and began to wade toward the wagon, rocking from side to side from the force of the flood. He reached the team, seized the bridle of the near horse and began to lead him to the shore. The frightened animal reared and fought, all but yanking Buckner off his feet, but the pressure of the water was in his favor, enabling him to stay upright and finally reach the embankment.

"Look out!"

At Martha Tallant's warning cry, Buckner twisted about. A large tree, its cluster of roots like a huge claw, was bearing down upon the wagon. It struck the right rear of the vehicle with tremendous force. The impact crushed the wheel, allowing the wagon to tilt dangerously.

"Jump!" Buckner yelled above the roar of the flood.

Through the rain he saw one of the women leave the wagon as he dragged himself along the side of the near horse. They had to be freed or else would drown. Feeling his way along the trace underwater, he unhooked the left and then the right from the singletree. Loose, the horse began to fight the water, all but knocking Buckner off his feet. Hanging on to the loose singletree, he managed to unhook the traces of the off-horse. The tongue had already come loose from the ring and both horses, free of the wagon's dead weight, instinctively began to head for the embankment.

Buckner came about. Augusta was in the water, struggling against the debris-laden current. Thalia, for one reason or another, had delayed. Something else struck the wagon. Buckner was unable to see what it was as he was fighting to keep his balance and go to Augusta's aid. He saw Thalia leap into the torrent at that moment, and at the same time caught sight through the rain-filled gloom of a log rushing toward her.

"Thalia!" he yelled, struggling to move. She did not hear him, he knew. The roaring and booming of the flood drowned out all else.

The log collided with her, driving her down into the surging, roily water. Buckner struck out against the strong current to reach the woman. She appeared briefly just ahead, her white face stark against the murky water. Buckner lunged forward. His fingers locked about an arm, and with all the strength he could muster, he drew her toward him. He glanced about for Augusta, saw that she had worked herself clear of the debris that had engulfed her and was climbing onto the shore.

Holding Thalia's limp body tight, Buckner began to fight his way against the powerful current to reach the embankment.

SEVENTEEN

FROM THE CORNER OF AN EYE Buckner saw the wagon swing out into the center of the rushing arroyo, the sounds of tearing canvas and crackling wood coming to him faintly above the roar of the storm. Struggling to keep his footing, with Thalia still unconscious, locked under his right arm, he pushed on through the swirling, chest deep water.

Clumps of brush dashed against him, caught momentarily on his clothing, and then swept on. Through the gray, wet haze he saw that Augusta had reached the embankment, and that Martha and Sibyl, arms outstretched, were helping her ashore. Lightning continued to flash, flooding the devastated scene with unnatural light which was followed almost instantly by deafening thunder.

The wagon, its canopy gone, rocked violently. With a sudden lurch it was caught up in the full force of the flooding current. As if some mighty hand had struck it broadside, it shot half out of the water, spilling its contents as it rose. For a fragment of time it seemed to be standing on end in the muddy, debris-filled arroyo, and then it toppled, ending bottom side up, unbroken wheels spinning furiously from the force of the current as it was carried on downstream.

Grim, muscles aching, Buckner looked ahead; a strong, muscular man, he was nevertheless losing the battle with the rushing, constantly rising water. Something under the surface struck his legs. He staggered, fought to stay upright as the women on shore screamed in fear. The bush or whatever it was tore free of his legs and whirled away. Buckner remained motionless for several moments until his footing was secure, then plunged on.

He reached the bank just as he thought his strength would forsake him. Martha and her two daughters took Thalia from him while at the same time helping him onto safe ground. Heaving a deep sigh, he sank onto the wet grass.

"Thalia! Thalia!" he heard Martha Tallant cry out as she sought to revive the young woman. "Oh, dear God—don't take her from me too!"

Buckner struggled to his feet. Maybe there was something he could do to help. Still sucking for wind, he made his way toward the dim, kneeling figures of the three women as they bent over the eldest sister.

"Thank you, God—thank you," he heard Martha say in a falling voice.

Thalia, supported by Sibyl and Augusta, was now sitting up. He could barely make out her features, chalk white in the rain-filled darkness, but she appeared to be dazed and uncertain of her whereabouts.

"Get her in the wagon," Buckner yelled, his mind again functioning logically. "She'll be all right. Main thing is we've got to get away from here—we've got to get on higher ground."

The women reacted immediately, and Buckner, moving past them, slipping and sliding with each step, made it to where Thalia's team stood wild-eyed and trembling near a small tree. Taking up the traces and other bits of hanging leather, he fastened them to the harness and then led the pair of Morgans to the rear of the wagon and securely tied them. The sorrel, as nervous as the team, was still attached, and leaving them he hurried around to the front of the vehicle and climbed aboard.

Augusta was on the seat. As she handed him the lines she ducked her head at the rear of the wagon bed. The wind had risen and the vehicle was rocking slightly back and forth.

"Thalia's all right. Just a hard knock on the head."

Buckner nodded. "Good. How about yourself?"

"I'm all right too. We owe you so much for—"

"Forget it," Buckner said, and released the brake. Shouting at the team, he put them into motion. The road was barely visible, but aided by the constant flashes of lightning, he was able to follow the rutted tracks.

"Sure sorry about the other wagon," he said after they had gotten underway.

Augusta, her yellow hair dark from rain and plastered to her head, managed a wry smile. Despite her general appearance and the strain showing in her face, she was pretty.

"We've lost almost everything with it—clothing, food, other supplies—even our musical instruments."

"A tough deal all right," he said. "I might have saved the wagon if that stump hadn't hit it, broke the wheel. But I guess we ought to figure ourselves lucky that we got across with this wagon, and without somebody getting hurt—or drowned."

"It was a close call for Thalia—"

"Are you sure she's all right? We can stop a little farther on up the road if you like!"

Augusta turned, yelled back into the wagon bed to her mother. They held a brief conversation, and the middle sister brought her attention back to Buckner.

"Mama says to stop when you think it's safe, then she'll

see to Thalia. And she'd like to talk to you when you can spare the time."

Buckner nodded as he strained to see the road ahead. The rain had slackened but the grayness persisted and he was having difficulty keeping the team and wagon in the ruts. Now and then it was necessary to swing out to avoid a washout.

"I'll pull up soon as I can," he said.

"Are you afraid those outlaws are somewhere behind us?"

"Can lay a bet on it. One thing in our favor, they'll have to hold off crossing that arroyo until it runs down, unless they managed to hit it about the same time as we did."

The rain continued to hammer at them, aided now by a rising wind that buffeted and rocked the wagon. Sibyl or Martha handed a blanket to Augusta. She crowded up close to Buckner, and, teeth chattering from the cold, draped the oblong of wool over the both of them. But what comfort the blanket provided—both were already soaked to the skin —was soon lost as it shortly became saturated with water.

A short time later, with the rain now slacking off, patches of moon and starlit sky began to appear. Buckner drew the team to a halt. The ground on either side of the road looked too soft and wet to support the wagon, so he simply remained in the more or less solid footing of the ruts.

Augusta exchanged places with her mother after the older woman had finished tending to her eldest daughter. Discarding the waterlogged blanket, she produced a thick, dry quilt. Laying it across their legs, she pulled it up as high as she could around their bodies to ward off the chill.

Settled, Martha said: "Sibyl told me she heard the out-laws say that my brother—Shad—was dead. Is that what you understood?"

"I heard it too," Buckner said. "There was another member of the bunch that rode in. Name was Bateman. He told the others that your brother up and died on him, was the way he put it. Was torturing him, I expect. Was after the money he was carrying."

Martha was silent for a few moments. "The money was to be my brother's share of our partnership."

"They seemed to know all about that. Reckon it explains why they jumped you—wanted your money, too." Buckner paused as a thought came to him. "Was it in the other wagon?"

Martha shook her head. In the dim light her features were soft and sad. "No, I'm carrying it on me—sewed in my clothing. And I have some of it in a money belt—"

"Mama—don't—" Augusta broke in. There was a note of warning in her voice.

Martha shrugged, drew the quilt closer about her shoulders. "After what he's been through for us I don't think we need to fear him—and we do need his help."

"What are we going to do?"

It was Thalia's voice. Buckner twisted about and looked at her. Wrapped in a blanket, she was immediately behind him. A white bandage was around her head. He remembered that he'd also been wearing a bandage, a souvenir of the encounter with the outlaws, but it had come loose and gotten lost sometime during the storm, he guessed.

"What else can we do but go on?" Martha replied.

"But with Uncle Shad dead, Papa gone, and losing about everything we own in that arroyo—"

"We still have each other, and we have enough money to go ahead with the ranch." Martha paused as lightning, well to the south, flared across the sky. "And if we decide a ranch isn't for us we can go into some kind of business—a hotel or maybe a restaurant. We can have that decided by the time we get to Colorado."

Martha Tallant was one hell of a woman, Buckner thought as he listened to her talk. Her husband and brother dead at the hands of outlaws, almost all of her possessions lost to a storm, and thousands of miles from home, she was still able to think of the future, and plan ahead for herself and her daughters.

"Getting there's not going to be easy, Mama—"

"I know that, Gussie. Seems nothing ever is, anymore. But Mr. Buckner said he'd stay with us, at least for a while."

There was a long quiet in which there were only the sounds of the diminishing rain and the weary stamp of one of the horses.

"It's what I was aiming to do," he said.

"We'll be happy to pay," Martha began, and hushed as he silenced her with a raised hand.

"I was brought up to never take pay for helping somebody."

"But what about those lawmen that are hunting you?" Augusta asked. "Aren't you afraid you'll run into them again?"

He shrugged. "Chance I'll have to take. They headed up this way so I'll have to keep an eye out. Last thing I want is for Henry Guzman to slap iron on me."

"Why, is he a bad lawman?"

"Got a reputation for being mighty hard—and he's got a special reason to nail me. He was in the bank when I collected my money. Expect he figures that was a real insult."

Sibyl, shivering visibly, laughed. Martha Tallant nodded. "I can see why he would take it personal . . . What do you think we should do now?"

"Keep going. This road will lead to somewhere, maybe connect with a main road that will take us on into Willow Springs and the Pass."

"Do you have any idea how far it might be? We don't have much food—the other wagon was carrying most of our supply," Martha said. "Do you think there will be a town or maybe a ranch along the way where we can buy provisions?"

"Probably will be," Buckner replied reassuringly, his tone belying his belief that the chances for such were so slim as to be practically none. "We'll make out. There ought to be plenty of game around here. Can take my rifle and go deer hunting, bring in some venison."

"Your rifle was in the other wagon," Augusta said. "So was the shotgun."

Buckner swore deeply under his breath, and then grinned. "I reckon it won't make no difference to a deer whether I kill him with a rifle or a six-gun. You all ready to move on?"

"I expect we are," Martha answered, glancing at the girls.

"Then we best pull out. Want everybody to keep an eye out for those outlaws. Be daylight soon and—"

"And we best watch for those lawmen, too," Thalia added.

Buckner nodded. "Right. They're both around somewhere."

EIGHTEEN

THE ROAD was slick and gullied in many places. Anything faster than a slow walk was out of the question, and conscious of the predicament the Tallant women would be in should they lose their last wagon, John Buckner drove the weary team with care.

The rain had passed on, relieving them of that minor worry. All were aware that the outlaws would not be giving up their determination to rob the Tallants of their money. And the fact they had not yet put in an appearance could be laid to the flooding arroyo and the difficulties they would have crossing it. But they would eventually catch up, and when that occurred Buckner's hope was that it would be in a place where he could make a successful stand.

He would need the breaks, that was certain. It would be one man with one gun against three, all well armed. The loss of his rifle and Thalia's shotgun was a serious matter and posed a handicap that could prove fatal unless he could manage somehow to even the odds.

"They were going to play cards for me," he heard Sibyl say in a voice that had a faint lift of pride in it.

"I expect you mean cut the cards," Augusta said. "It's whoever gets the highest card that wins."

"What about the young one that you said sort of looked after you? Was he in on that?"

"No, I don't think he was."

"You seem interested in him," Martha said, looking back into the wagon. "What's his name, do you know?"

"Ben—Ben Tolliver. One of the other men is his father."

"Well, just you don't forget he's one of the bunch that killed Papa!" Thalia said in an angry voice.

"He was with them all right," Sibyl explained, "but he told me that when he saw all us women in the wagons he fired his gun into the ground so's he wouldn't hit one of us."

The front wheels of the wagon dropped into a deep cut in the road that Buckner had failed to see in the poor light, and lurching forward, silencing conversation for several moments, Buckner, getting the vehicle leveled off, studied the country ahead in the slowly lightening gloom for a place to pull up.

"You believe that?" Thalia asked in a wondering tone.

"I—I'm not sure. I think I do. He doesn't seem like one of them. He was more like us, like just ordinary folks."

"He's an outlaw," Thalia stated bluntly. "Nothing you can say will change that."

"The sun's coming up!" Martha Tallant announced, her voice reflecting a mixture of joy and relief. "Now maybe we'll get a chance to dry out."

Buckner turned his eyes to the east. It was the false dawn; it would be a half hour or so before the sun showed itself on the horizon—and not then unless a bank of heavy clouds hanging low in the gray sky drifted away.

"I figure to stop when we come to a good place," he said. "If there's any grub we can cook up a breakfast."

"We don't have much, that's for sure," Martha said. "Maybe you could go deer hunting first thing."

"Plan to. I saw a sack of oats for the horses in the back. Can boil up a pot of it."

Sibyl made a noise of distaste at the suggestion. The older woman turned to her. "That very well may be all we'll have to eat, young lady, so don't go turning your nose up on it!"

"But, Mama—oats! That's what we feed horses. I'd rather go hungry."

"Could be you'll change your tune if we can't find anything else," Augusta said as the team plodded slowly up a slight grade.

They were entering a more mountainous area, leaving the low hills behind. Buckner continued to search for a suitable place to pull off as well as keeping an eye out for the outlaws and Henry Guzman. He wasn't too concerned about the latter; that the detective was farther north, possibly even in Colorado by that hour, was only logical.

They were moving through tall pines and firs, but not yet in aspen and spruce country, and despite the clearing sky, it was still half dark. There was considerable thick brush growing along the roadway, and Buckner felt a mounting uneasiness; the area was not to his liking. If the outlaws jumped them anywhere along the road, he would have little chance.

"Will we be able to stop soon?" Augusta asked, leaning forward over the back of the seat.

"It's up to Mr. Buckner," Martha replied. "He knows best."

Buckner shifted, shook his head. "It sure would oblige me if you'd all call me John. Can't get used to this Mister thing."

The girls laughed. Martha smiled. "All right, John, that's how it will be. You already know our names so you must use them."

"Fair enough," Buckner said, his attention now on the road ahead.

A quarter mile or so he could see the vague, slanting shape of a rockslide. A little of the tension faded from his rugged features. It could be the place he was looking for—one where he could make a stand when the outlaws showed up. Once more he checked the country around them for any sign of Bateman and the Tollivers, and was relieved to find none.

"I expect our names sound odd to you," he heard Sibyl say. "Papa picked them. He was once a schoolteacher—back in Massachusetts when he was young. He took them from the classics."

"I reckon a name's a name no matter where it came from," Buckner said. "Can say this about all of yours, however—they're mighty pretty."

Sibyl thanked him, Augusta and Thalia quiet as the wagon again thudded into a deep rut and bounded out once more, and both laughed.

"I took a lot of joshing about mine," the older sister said. "Other children at school were always making up rhymes to go with it."

"I had the same problem. I was called July or December or some other month—never August—"

"I'm sure John isn't interested in all this," Martha said. "And we certainly have more important and serious things to think about."

"We're sorry, Mama," Sibyl said quickly, laying a hand on her mother's shoulder. "I guess we forgot about the bad fix we're in."

"Fix is certainly the right word for it," the older woman said.

"But we'll make out," Thalia said. "Isn't that right, John?"

"Expect it is," he answered, beginning to swing off the

road toward the rockslide. "Just a matter of making do with what we've got."

The small flat at the foot of the rockslide was much to his liking. He was able to drive the wagon in close, thus making it impossible for the outlaws or Guzman and his posse to get in behind them. There was grass available for the horses, wood for a fire, but there was no creek nearby to furnish water, making it necessary for them to rely on the big five-gallon galvanized milk cans the family carried in the wagon for such times, and a sinkhole filled by the rains would provide for the horses.

Pulling to a stop, Buckner immediately dropped to the ground, and after first making sure there were no signs of the outlaws or the posse, he began to unhitch the team.

"I'll see what we can do about something to eat," Martha said as he unhooked the singletrees. "Do you have anything in your saddlebags or that grub sack?"

"Some dry biscuits and a little coffee," he replied. "You'll find a frying pan and a lard tin that I've been using to cook with."

"Good. A fire will be all right, won't it?"

He nodded. "That bunch knows we headed up the road. Be no trouble to follow our tracks. A fire sure won't be giving us away."

Martha nodded. "I'll put Sassy to finding dry wood. The other girls can help me. Is there a chance you can get some meat? I think you said something about a deer."

"Figured to set snares for rabbits soon as I get the horses looked after. Not hoping much for a deer—a six-gun's hardly big enough to bring one down. Takes a rifle or a shotgun—"

"I know. It's too bad we lost the other wagon," the woman said, and turned back into the wagon, where her daughters were going through the boxes and bags in search of supplies.

Buckner resumed the chore of freeing the team, turned the harness up into itself, and after leading the pair of weary Morgans to a grassy area near the sink, returned for the sorrel and the other team. The gelding he tethered to one of the pines with a fairly long rope while he considered what was best to do with the second team. He thought of hobbling the animals but decided that, with their harness on, and worn as they were, it was unlikely they would stray far from the others. Besides, he and the women would always be close by to watch over them.

The horses cared for, and in the brightening day, he returned to the camp, where the women were making things ready. Martha Tallant had gotten into the sack of oats, placed a quart or so in a bucket, and added water.

"I'm hoping we'll be able to eat this after it has cooked a bit," she said. "What are you looking for?"

Buckner, poking about in the wagon bed, paused and looked over his shoulder. "Cord—of some kind. Need it to make snares."

Martha pointed to a basket hanging from the forward bow. "You'll find some fishing line in there. Will it do?"

"Be just what I need," Buckner said, and reached up into the wicker container. Feeling about, he came up with the line which had been wound about a bit of wood.

With the oiled cord in hand he glanced about for the area where he'd most likely find rabbits. Off a short way he could see Sibyl probing about under the trees and bushes for dry wood, stopping occasionally to break off a dead limb and add it to the supply being carried in her apron.

Augusta was in the wagon with her mother, and Thalia was building a firebox by arranging stones in a circle. Moving up to her, he said, "Going after rabbits. Don't aim to go far so if anybody shows up, sing out."

The woman shrugged. She was still far from friendly, he realized as he walked on toward a thickly overgrown slope below the camp. She still had her suspicions but he'd not hold it against her; it was only natural.

When he got to the dense stand of berry bushes, false sage and other low shrubs, Buckner began to look for runs and other traces of rabbits. He found a hole almost immediately, cut off a length of the cord, and fashioned a slip-knot loop at one end. After attaching the other end to the limb of a nearby sapling, he pulled the branch down and held it in a cocked position by placing a small piece of wood between it and the tree's trunk. Then he opened the noose the width of the narrow passageway through the brush and lightly anchored the sides so that the loop would remain open.

Stepping back, Buckner rechecked his efforts. A slight pull on the noose would dislodge the bit of wood that served as a trigger, and the limb would swing back into place. Satisfied the trap was well set, he moved on.

A few yards farther along he located a second warren, and set up a similar snare. As he straightened up to work deeper into the thicket, Buckner froze. Standing before him no more than ten feet away was a young deer—a buck whose spike antlers were still in velvet.

The animal was as startled at the unexpected confrontation as was Buckner, but John reacted more swiftly. He drew his .44 instantly and fired twice. The deer staggered and fell.

Scarcely believing his good fortune, Buckner hurried to the buck's side prepared to fire another bullet if it weren't dead. The deer represented food for the Tallants and himself until they reached Willow Springs, still several days away, judging from the ragged line of hazy blue mountains well to the north. There was no need for a third shot. He grasped the buck by its short antlers and headed back for camp.

A faint regret coursed through him as he slowly made his

way through the dense growth. Anyone on the mountain-side and in the nearby canyons could have heard the gun-shots. That Bateman and the Tollivers would now have a good idea of their whereabouts had to be admitted. The same was true of Henry Guzman and his men if they had not gone on north but circled back and were somewhere in the vicinity. Buckner shrugged. He'd had no choice in the matter; he had to provide food for the Tallant women and himself, and it was either use his gun or allow the deer to get away.

As he broke out of the tangle of brush dragging the buck behind him, the four women, faces stiff with anxiety, for-sook what they were doing and hurried toward him.

"Thank heaven you're all right!" Martha Tallant cried. "When we heard those shots we—"

"It's a deer!" Augusta shouted. "John's shot a deer! Now we will have meat to eat."

Buckner grinned. "Sorry the shooting scared you but it was the only way I could bring him down."

Beyond Martha he could see Thalia smiling at him, and beside her Sibyl was staring at the buck, the sadness of a youngster viewing a wild creature no longer alive on her soft features.

"I'll dress him out and we can eat venison steaks for supper," Buckner said, continuing on to camp.

"And we can roast what's left and have meat to eat when-ever we want it," Martha said happily. "Oh, I wish there was some way to keep the heart and liver from spoiling."

They reached the camp, a panorama of color from the clothing, quilts and blankets hung out to dry in the warm sun. Still uneasy about the outlaws and possibly Guzman hearing the gunshots, Buckner dragged the buck to a nearby pine, and with a bit of rope from the wagon, hauled the carcass up to where he could more easily work on it.

"It'll take a while to fry steaks with that small spider of

yours," Martha said, coming over to assist him. "When you cut them, it might be a good idea to make them small."

"Can roast some and fry some," Buckner said, reaching for his knife. He froze. In the brush and trees on the far side of the road he had seen movement. A moment later the picture clarified itself. Three horses.

"All of you!" he called in a hoarse whisper as he started for the wagon in a run. "Get over here with me—it's those outlaws!"

NINETEEN

MARTHA TALLANT immediately whirled about. She saw the direction in which Buckner was looking, and instantly started toward the wagon.

"Girls!" she called in an urgent voice. "Hurry!"

Thalia joined her quickly. She was followed almost at once by Augusta. Breathless, they reached the wagon.

"What is it?" Augusta asked.

"Those outlaws," the older woman replied. "Oh, why won't they leave us be?"

"Long as you've got that money they'll never back off," Buckner said. "Want you all to get in the wagon. Stay down low. The sides of the bed will stop a bullet, I think." He paused as the women began to hurriedly climb aboard. "Where's the young one—Sibyl?"

Martha's face went chalk white. "I—I thought she—"

"Here she comes," Thalia cut in.

Sibyl reached the wagon, clambered up a front wheel and crowded into the back with the others.

"Where were you?" Martha demanded, angry lines now deepening her features.

"I know where she was," Augusta said before the younger girl could answer. "I saw her below here a little bit before John killed that deer. It looked like she was talking to someone."

Buckner was only half listening. His attention, now that all of the women were safe inside the wagon, was on the trees and brush on the far side of the road where he had spotted the outlaws.

It could be Guzman and the posse, he thought, and not the outlaws. But he doubted that. Hunched low, he moved away from the wagon to make a stand behind one of the larger pines. It could even be nothing more than some cowhands heading north in search of work.

"Who were you talking to, Sibyl?" he heard Martha Tallant demand in a severe voice. "Was it that young outlaw you seem to have taken a shine to?"

Sibyl's reply was low and Buckner could barely make it out. It was Ben Tolliver. That immediately answered the question of who the riders he'd seen were. A gunshot ripped the late morning quiet. Buckner, crouched behind the big pine, listened to the weapon's echoing report as he tried to locate its source. Whoever had fired the gun was across the road among the brush and trees, he knew, but exactly where was the puzzle.

A thin, small cloud of smoke no larger than a water bucket drifted upward from a thicket of small trees directly opposite. Buckner immediately snapped a shot at the cluster, rose, made a break for a rocky, brush-covered mound a dozen strides nearer to the road.

Guns hammered instantly. He could hear the whine of bullets and see the spurts of damp earth around him as, running at full speed, he began to weave from side to side. A tall figure materialized along the edge of the road. Bateman! The outlaw had a rifle in his hands and was sighting along its rusty barrel.

John Buckner, not breaking stride, triggered two quick shots at the hulking shape. Bateman yelled and staggered as the lead smashed into him. He tried to bring the rifle back up but strength failed him. His arms came down and the weapon fell to the ground. For a long minute the outlaw stood weaving uncertainly in the dappled sunlight, and then abruptly collapsed.

Buckner reached the rocky hillock and threw himself in behind the highest point. The Tollivers were somewhere near Bateman, he felt sure. Suddenly one of the remaining outlaws opened up from the stand of saplings where he had first spotted gunsmoke. In the protection of the rocks, Buckner flung three shots at Tolliver hiding among the trees. As answering shots came, he thumbed fresh cartridges from his gun belt and reloaded. Guessing what was taking place, the outlaw increased his barrage of lead after changing from handgun to rifle.

Now, the .44 fully loaded, Buckner backed away from his position on the ragged mound and began to work his way, flat on his belly, around it. He was hoping that the lifting gunsmoke would give away Tolliver's position just as it had that of Bateman earlier. The idea was a good one. Just as he reached the forward edge of the pile he saw not only smoke but Pete Tolliver as well.

The outlaw, crouched low, was moving toward a clump of thick brush growing along the edge of the road. Buckner drew his legs up under his taut body and came partly erect.

"Tolliver!" he yelled. His gun was up and ready.

The outlaw spun. Both men fired simultaneously. John Buckner felt the searing shock as a bullet drove into the fleshy part of his leg. He went to one knee, seeing in that same instant Pete Tolliver go down. The outlaw triggered his gun once more at Buckner but it was mere reflex and the bullet caromed noisily off a nearby rock and went screaming into space.

Ignoring the pain in his leg, Buckner struggled to his feet. There was still Ben Tolliver to account for. Movement among the trees caught his attention. He fired instantly, saw it was one of the outlaw horses, riderless, shying nervously about in the smoky confusion. Hunkering low, he awaited the answering shot from Ben. There was only the distant cawing of crows passing, winging their way to some favorite resting place, and the forlorn coo of a wild pigeon back up the slope somewhere.

Tension began to die within Buckner and the hollow, empty feeling that always came after a shootout in which he'd been a reluctant, if victorious, participant. He had killed few men in his life, even during the war, and it was something in which he took no pride. He pulled off his still rain-damp neckerchief and bound it around his leg to stop the flow of blood, then turned and started back to the camp. Evidently Ben Tolliver had wanted none of the shootout.

The women saw him coming, and at once piled out of the wagon and headed for him. Thalia was the first to reach him. Tears were glistening in her eyes as she halted.

"You're hurt," she murmured, throwing her arm about his shoulder to support his faltering step.

He stared at her, not understanding her show of concern. Up to that time she had been the one who had remained the most aloof and wary.

"Yeh, got myself nicked," he said as Martha and Augusta drew up beside them, both breathing heavily from the running. The older woman glanced off to the wooded area on the far side of the road.

"The outlaws—are they—"

"They won't bother you again," he replied. "Leastwise two of them won't. The other one, the boy—I never saw him."

"I doubt if you or any of us ever will," Augusta said. "He was over by those trees below camp. And"—she paused and looked at her mother—"Sibyl ran to him. I called to her but she didn't pay any mind."

"You mean she went with him?" Martha Tallant asked in a heavy, resigned voice.

"I guess so, Mama. I turned to see what you all were doing, and then when I looked back they were gone."

Buckner swore quietly. "Let's get my leg patched up so's I can ride, and I'll go after them."

Martha was silent for a long breath. She shook her head. "Sibyl's not much more than a child, but she's old enough to know her own mind. Let her go."

TWENTY

WALKING SLOWLY and painfully, with Thalia supporting him on one side, Buckner returned to camp. Martha, lips set tight and grimly quiet, hurried on ahead with Augusta.

"Get some water to heating," he heard the older woman say. "That wound will need cleaning and disinfecting. It's a good thing we didn't move the medicine chest to the other wagon, too."

"Your mama's going to a lot of trouble," Buckner muttered to Thalia. "I've been hurt worse branding a steer."

"Maybe," Thalia said, "but you've lost a lot of blood. Anyway, Mama knows best."

Buckner slanted a glance at the girl. At that moment she appeared even more beautiful than he had noticed. The blue of her eyes had taken on a softness, and her dark hair, bared to the now brightly shining sun, had a faint red tinge to it, while her brows, full and thick, looked to be jet black. The curve of her jaw rounded out her tanned features nicely, lending a strong but womanly look to her face.

He hoped she was having kinder thoughts toward him, that she was becoming as attracted to him as he was to her. Never before had he felt about any woman the way he did Thalia, but he reckoned he might as well forget that. She was being nice to him because of the confrontation with the outlaws and the fact he'd gotten himself shot. Thalia Tallant was of a different world; well educated, talented, and with beauty fortified by strength and character, what would she see in him? He was no more than a drifter, a farmer turned saddle-tramp, a wanted criminal and a killer who had cut down three men in the last few hours.

His musings came to an end. They had reached the camp and Martha was motioning him to a boulder where he was to sit while she took care of his wound.

"The water will be hot in a minute," the older woman said, kneeling before him. Removing the neckerchief, she handed it to Thalia. "Wash it in cold water so the blood won't set," she directed, and looked up at Buckner.

"Shall I cut your pants or do you want to slip them off? I have to get to the wound." She paused, smiled. "Don't worry about embarrassing me—I've been married a good many years."

Buckner grinned, and released his gun belt. Laying it aside within easy reach, he unhooked his pants' clasp and pushed his trousers down to where the woman could get at the bullet wound.

"I don't figure it's bad," he said. "Missed the bone, cut a track through the flesh."

"Still bleeding some," Martha said, and dipping a cloth pad in the hot water, began to dab at the wound. When it was cleaned to her satisfaction she applied the disinfectant, added some salve, and then wrapped a bandage about the leg.

"That will do for a spell," Martha said, getting to her feet. "I'll look at it again tomorrow."

"Sure obliged," Buckner replied. He drew his pants back into place and tongued the belt.

"Like you said, it wasn't a bad wound. Another inch to the side and the bullet would have missed entirely."

Buckner reached down, took up his gun belt, and strapped the .44 about his waist. Martha frowned.

"What are you going to do? You shouldn't—"

"Aim to dress out that buck," he said, and ignoring her protest, crossed to where the deer was hanging.

Martha said nothing further but shortly joined him, and together they skinned the young buck, skillfully removed the internal organs without breaking the sack, and within another hour had the carcass quartered for slicing into roasts and steaks. That would require another hour, but before he had completed the task Martha and her two daughters had meat cooking over the fire.

"We best roast the other quarters," Buckner said when he was finished. "It'll keep them from spoiling."

"We found a little salt in your grub sack, but not enough to salt down the meat. I just wish we had some flour and lard. Those oat cakes would taste a lot better."

Buckner glanced at the small pads of softened grain cooking on a piece of flat metal the women had found in the wagon. They were browning from the heat and giving off a good odor.

"They'll do fine," he said, taking his freshly washed neckerchief from the stick near the fire where Thalia had hung it to dry. Returning it to its place about his neck, he nodded to the young woman.

"Obliged to you. Expect it's the first time it's been cleaned since I bought it in Wichita."

Thalia smiled and pointed to his bullet-torn, blood-stained pants. "They need cleaning and mending, too."

He shook his head. "I'm thanking you but we won't bother. First creek we come to I'll wade out and let them clean themselves."

"Which reminds me of something I need to tell you," Augusta said. The small steaks were almost done and the odor of frying meat filled the air and heightened the hun-

ger pains besetting them all, "We're running out of water.
The milk can is almost empty."

Martha turned to Buckner. "Is there a stream or a river
anywhere close?"

He stirred, shifted his weight to his uninjured leg. "Sure
don't know. Rode north a couple of times but never
through this part—was farther east. But I expect we'll come
across a creek somewhere ahead. We're getting nearer to
the high mountains."

"I've noticed that," Thalia said, gazing off into the direction where a line of towering peaks filled the distant horizon. "Is that Colorado?"

"That's it. Once we get over the Pass, we'll be there.
That venison smells mighty good."

"It's ready," Augusta said, and using a pointed stick for a
fork, speared one of the small steaks and handed it to him.
"It'll be hot!"

It was, but Buckner, hungry as he was, did not mind. He
juggled it back and forth between his hands briefly, and
then began to eat. The oat cakes, also ready, were tasteless
but filling, and coffee, passed around in the lone cup
Martha had found in Buckner's grub sack, gave the meal a
final touch.

When it was over and their hunger had been satisfied,
Buckner crossed to the wagon. His leg pained him and he
limped badly, but he had a chore to do. The sooner he took
care of it the better he would feel.

"I hope Sibyl has something to eat," he heard Martha
Tallant say as she added fuel to the fire. It would take most
of the night to roast what was left of the deer.

"She'll be all right, Mama," Augusta said. "Sassy's a lot
more grown up than you think."

"Are you looking for something?"

At Thalia's question Buckner, rummaging about in the

wagon, turned. He hadn't noticed that she had followed him.

"Yes, a shovel. I've got some burying to do."

"I see—those outlaws," she murmured, and pointed to a far corner. "Look behind that box. You'll find a spade there."

He did as directed and produced a short-handled round-pointed implement. "This'll do fine," he said as he backed out of the wagon.

"I'll help," Thalia said. "I'll get a blanket to wrap them in."

After telling Martha what they intended to do, they crossed the road to where the bodies of the two men lay. Locating a gully, Buckner deepened it a bit, and with the help of Thalia brought up the corpses. He spread the blanket in the hollow, laid the bodies side by side and folded the wool cover over them. As he climbed out of the depression Thalia began to fill in the grave. He took the spade from her and finished the job, then, to complete the task, they gathered up what rocks they could find and piled them onto the mound.

Leaning on the spade, he brushed at the sweat beading his forehead, aware as he did that Thalia was studying him thoughtfully.

"Something on your mind?"

She smiled faintly. "Just occurred to me not many men would go to the trouble of burying a couple of outlaws, especially when they had tried their best to kill him."

"Couldn't leave them laying out there for the coyotes and the buzzards to get at." He paused, again shifted his weight to ease the pain in his leg. "They were men, no matter who or what they did. Deserved to be buried."

"That sounds strange coming from you. I—I thought maybe you might enjoy killing, but I see I was wrong. If you did you'd not go to all this trouble."

"You've got me wrong. I haven't killed many men, only those like these two where I had no choice. It was either cut them down or they'd put me under. Only hope that when a bullet comes along with my name on it, somebody'll be kind enough to bury me."

He glanced up to the sky. Dark clouds were beginning to gather again, and the promise of rain, mingling with the smell of already wet juniper, was in the air.

"Expect we best be getting back. More rain coming."

Thalia stepped over to face him squarely. "I'm sorry if I said the wrong thing about you're being a—about you killing men. I didn't know that—"

"Forget it," he said. "Folks have a habit of pinning a label on a man whether he deserves it or not. And if it's the wrong kind of a label, it's just his tough luck."

"I understand," Thalia murmured. "Are we moving on today?"

"No, figure we're all due a good night's rest. Same goes for the horses. Best we get everything all set and pull out at first light in the morning."

"How far are we from the Pass, from the town of Willow Springs I think you called it."

"Still not sure," he replied, looking around for landmarks. "Don't think it'll be much more than four, maybe five days. Switching teams like I aim to do will let us travel faster since the horses will be fresh . . . What about your sister—Sibyl? You think your mama meant what she said about letting her go?"

"I guess she did—"

"We could stay over another day. I'd get on my horse and scout around, see if I could find her."

Thalia shook her head. "No, Mama wouldn't let you do that. Like she said, Sassy's old enough to know what she wants, and if she wants that kind of life, all well and good."

"It could be a hard one for her," Buckner said. "Need to

check those rabbit snares I put out. Maybe we'll have something beside venison to eat."

"I'm grateful we have that," Thalia replied.

The rain started again around the middle of the afternoon, falling lightly and causing no particular inconvenience. They had a late supper, this time varied by the meat of the two rabbits the snares had captured. They were also able to replenish their water supply a bit by trapping rain on a tarp and draining it into the milk can. Not long before the first signs of daylight they were up, had a breakfast of weak coffee, since the grounds had already been used once, venison and oat cakes, and were on their way.

On the second day out, Thalia, riding the sorrel in order to alleviate the crowding in the wagon, doubled back from scouting ahead and reported that a pilgrim, headed in the opposite direction, was around the next bend.

It proved to be a family of four—husband, wife, and two young sons—from Nebraska on their way to Las Vegas, New Mexico Territory, where they planned to start a new life.

"Name's Denison," the pilgrim said as he and Buckner exchanged handshakes. "Where you headed?"

For the first time in several hours John Buckner thought of Henry Guzman and the posse that had trailed him all the way from Missouri and were somewhere ahead. He glanced at Martha and her daughters. They were in conversation with Denison's wife. He turned back to the Nebraskan, a big, rawboned, red-faced man in overalls, cotton undershirt, straw hat and sodbuster shoes.

"How far are we from the Pass?"

Denison scratched at his jaw. "Two days, more or less. More if we get some weather. How is it on ahead?"

"Been raining aplenty. You'll have to watch for washouts." He paused as all four women followed by the two boys came to the back of the wagon. "Much going on in Willow Springs?"

"Talking railroad—everybody, seems—"

"John," Martha said, "I've been doing some trading. We're giving the Denisons a quarter of the venison for some things we need."

"Is it a hind quarter?" Denison asked before Buckner could comment.

"It is—"

"Good enough. We stocked up on just about everything but meat while we were there," Denison said. "They just didn't have nothing fit to buy. Hell, some of it I wouldn't give a dog."

Martha carried out her trading with Denison's wife, whose name proved to be Ruby, while the men discussed topics familiar to them. After an hour or so the bargaining was all done and they parted and continued on their respective ways.

"Just think, John, we won't have to live on just venison now!" Martha exulted. "We have flour, lard, some potatoes and onions, salt, a little sugar, and some chicory coffee. Ruby even gave me a couple of pans she never uses.

"Oh, I'm so glad we ran into the Denisons! Ruby and I became good friends. We promised to write each other as soon as we're settled. And we're only two days from town, she said."

"Is that right?" Augusta asked, face brightening.

"That's what her husband told me," Buckner said.

The women were excited at the thought not only of having food other than deer meat, but at reaching civilization, and their exuberance brushed aside all thoughts that Buckner had about Henry Guzman and the two men with him. That they could be in Willow Springs was, of course, a possibility, but he still felt the detective would have gone on, pressing the pursuit into Colorado.

"Is there a hotel in the town?" Augusta wondered. "It would be so good to sleep in a bed again!"

"And get a bath," Martha added. "It seems ages since I actually bathed."

"Well, the town's not much—leastwise it wasn't the last time I was there, but there was an inn where you could put up," Buckner said. "Had a room where you could take a bath, too."

"And a restaurant, I hope," Thalia said.

She was riding alongside the wagon, a habit she had acquired the second day after leaving camp. They had grown closer, she sitting next to him on the seat when Augusta took her turn riding the sorrel, and at night when the meal was over, they could be found, side by side, in front of the fire, talking or staring into the flames, oftentimes after Martha and Augusta had retired.

"There's a couple of them in Willow. Teamsters are big eaters," Buckner assured her.

They camped that night on the crest of a hill that overlooked a long, seemingly endless plain. The day had ended beautifully in a blaze of vivid color that filled the sky. The rain had ceased early that morning, and it was comfortably warm despite the altitude. As they were finishing supper Martha turned to him.

"Have you thought of what you will do if that detective is waiting for you in Willow Springs?"

Buckner reached for his cigarette makings, realized he had been out for days, and shook his head. "It's come to mind a few times. Not sure he'll even be there, but if—"

"If—" Thalia prompted when his words broke off.

"Reckon I'll just have to go along with him. Can't risk any shooting."

"Because of us—that what you mean?" Augusta asked.

Buckner's shoulders stirred. "Mostly. There's other reasons, too."

The subject died there. Later when he was alone in his blanket near the fire John Buckner considered his reply. He had vowed to himself long ago to never let Guzman or any other lawman take him in for a crime that, in his mind, he had not committed. But now things were different. The Tallant women—particularly Thalia—had changed his outlook.

He was still thinking about it that next day when they crossed the last flat and turned into the town's main street. If all went well he would see the women not only to Willow Springs, but over the Pass into Colorado. Then on to the ranch they were planning to buy—if that was still Martha's intention. At that point, if he could muster enough courage he would ask Thalia to marry him.

"We're here!" he heard Augusta say in a relieved tone. "There were times when I wondered if we—"

"Far enough, Buckner!" a hard voice cut into her happy words. "Pull up right where you are!"

Guzman! Buckner's hand dropped automatically to the butt of the .44 on his hip, and slowly fell away. Thalia, beside him on the seat, gasped. As the team came to a stop he handed her the lines and raised his hands.

"All right, Detective. No gunplay."

Guzman, stepping out from behind the end building along the street, moved into the center of the muddy roadway.

"Be no shooting unless you start it," he said evenly. "Now, step down, slow and easy. You're under arrest."

TWENTY-ONE

"NO!" THALIA CRIED in a sudden, anguished voice. "You can't do this!"

Guzman considered her coldly. "Lady, I am doing it. I don't know what he's told you, but you best keep out of it."

"He had a right to do what he did," Martha Tallant said, moving up to the back of the seat where she could be seen. "John is a good and honest man. He proved that by helping us."

"Means nothing. All I'm interested in is getting him back to Missouri to face bank robbery charges."

"But he didn't rob any bank—" Thalia protested. "It was his money and—"

Buckner laid a broad hand on the young woman's arm. "No use talking to him. He's got his mind set and there'll be no changing it. I'll try to convince the judge—"

"You climbing down?" Guzman broke in, waggling the pistol he was holding.

"There'll be no shooting here in the street!" a man wearing a deputy sheriff's star said, coming out from behind the same building. "And I ain't sure yet there's anything against this man. Got only what you've told me." He hesitated, averted his glance to Buckner. A tall, lean, sun-browned man with dark eyes and thin lips partly hidden by a mustache, he looked young for the job. "Your name John Buckner?"

"I reckon it is," Buckner said.

"Man here claims you robbed a bank back in some Missouri town, and that he was sent to collar you and take you back. That true?"

Buckner smiled tightly. "Guess part of it's true. Wasn't exactly that way."

"Then I expect you better step down and come along with me," the deputy said. "I'll have to keep you in the lockup till I get some authority from Missouri to turn you over to this fellow."

"Damn it, Lucas—I showed you my credentials!" Guzman shouted angrily.

"You did, for a fact," Lucas admitted, "but you never showed me any authority telling me to turn this man over to you. Now, I ain't figuring on doing so until I get word that it's all right."

"Hell, that could take days!" Guzman fumed. "The sheriff was out of town when I started chasing this outlaw. Could still be gone."

"Then we'll just have to wait," Lucas said, and beckoned to Buckner. "Climb down, mister—and do it right. I don't want no trouble."

Buckner felt Thalia's fingers tighten about his arm. He turned, smiled at her.

"Don't worry, I'll be all right," he said. He gingerly threw his legs over the side of the wagon, stepped onto the wheel and lowered himself to the ground.

"You hurt?" Lucas asked, frowning.

"Nothing special," Buckner replied indifferently. If the deputy learned about the shootout with the outlaws, he could be in for a lengthy session of questioning.

"I'll take that iron you're wearing," Lucas said, and lifted

Buckner's six-gun from its holster and thrust it under his belt. "Jail's right on down the street."

Buckner nodded. "Be obliged if you'll let me talk to my womenfolk for a bit. I won't give you any trouble."

"Go ahead," Lucas said. "You've got two minutes."

Buckner turned back to the wagon. The Tallants, Thalia, Martha and Augusta, now off the sorrel, looked down at him. Their faces were stiff and strained from anxiety.

"You go get yourselves a room at the inn," he said. "There'll be a stable behind it where the horses can be looked after. I'll come soon as I can."

"Not likely," Henry Guzman said dryly. "You're as good as in the Grovertown jail right now."

Buckner glanced at the detective and grinned. "Whatever you say, Detective," he murmured. He winked at Thalia, came about and moved off down the street with Deputy Sheriff Lucas.

A dozen or so onlookers had gathered to view the proceedings. All stared at John Buckner curiously as, limping slightly, he passed. Some were smiling.

"Got yourself a prisoner, eh, Lucas?" one commented. "Well, hang onto him, boy."

"Go to hell," the lawman replied, and pointed to a building with barred windows sitting apart from its neighbors a short distance to the left. "That's where we're going," he added to Buckner.

"When did you send word to the sheriff in Grovertown?" Buckner asked as they drew up to the door.

"Been a few days ago," Lucas replied. "The detective said he had a hunch you were headed this way. Seems he was right."

"And you'll damn soon find out I've got the authority to take him back to Missouri, too!" Guzman said, wiping the sweat from his florid features.

"We'll see," Lucas said mildly, pushing Buckner through

the doorway. He pointed to one of the three cells lined across the rear of the building. All were empty. "Get in one of them and set yourself down."

The full impact of his situation did not hit John Buckner until the barred door of his cell clanged shut and the deputy turned the key in the lock. He had never been in jail before and the thought of being shut in for even a day chilled his blood. And if Guzman got him back to Missouri and was successful in having him put away in the state's prison for years . . .

Hunched on the slatted cot in his cell, Buckner rolled his predicament about in his head. He'd never let it come down to that; Henry Guzman would never make it back to Grovertown with him—he'd guarantee that! Meanwhile he'd have to make some arrangements for Thalia and her mother and sister. He doubted they would want to go on to Colorado now. With both her husband and brother dead, and with him unable to help them further, she would likely have a change of plans. He'd see if Lucas would let him talk matters over with the women. Too, he wanted to see Thalia again.

She had come to mean much to him in those last few days, and he was fairly certain the interest was mutual. He could now forget his plans to go on to Colorado with the family, and ask her to be his wife, however. That would have to wait—at least for a while. Buckner glanced up as Guzman entered the jail. Not the detective or anyone else was going to keep Thalia and him apart—not unless she wanted it that way, he vowed silently.

"Here's your message," he heard Guzman say as he walked up to the desk where Lucas was sitting. "Was over at the stage office when it come in. Thought I'd save them the trouble of delivering it."

"Was mighty kind of you," the deputy said in an icy tone. He opened the message and read its brief contents, then glanced up at the detective. "This here's your authority, all right. But I reckon you've already seen it."

"Didn't need to see it," Guzman snapped. "Knew I had it all the time. Was only that you—"

"You saying you knew didn't mean nothing to me. I had to have it down in black and white," Lucas said. "When do you aim to pull out?"

"In the morning," the detective said. "If them two jaspers that was with me had waited another day we could've all gone back together, but no, they just couldn't hold off."

"Never seen a posse yet that wasn't wanting to quit before the job was done," Lucas said, his tone now a bit more civil. "What do you want me to do with the money I took out of the prisoner's saddlebags?"

As Buckner had expected, they had found the money. He still had a small amount on him as Lucas hadn't bothered to have him empty his pockets.

"I'll be taking it right along with me."

Lucas scratched his head. "You think that's smart? Lot of cash for a man to be carrying, and it sure is a fair piece to Missouri."

"Don't you fret none about that. I'll get it back to Grovertown, same as I will him," Guzman said. "Just you have him ready to ride in the morning—along with the money."

Lucas stiffened slightly at the detective's imperious tone, and then shrugged. "They'll be ready."

"Good," Guzman said, and left the jail.

"Deputy—" Buckner called.

"Yeh?"

"What Guzman there told you about me's not exactly the way of it. I—"

"Ain't no use talking to me about it now. I got my orders when that message came, so my hands are tied. Can say

howsomever, that I'm inclined to lean your way after talking to your women."

"Appreciate that. But—"

"Best thing you can do is hope for a fair trial back there
in Missouri. You figure you'll get it?"

"As fair as I'd get anywhere, I expect. I'd like to ask a
favor."

"Ask—"

"I'm worried about the women—they've been through
hell. I'd like to talk to them for a few minutes."

"Sure don't see why not," Lucas said cheerfully. "I'll
fetch them after supper."

TWENTY-TWO

IT WAS WELL AFTER DARK and a good two hours since he'd been served his supper, brought to him by one of the women who worked in the restaurant at the inn, when John Buckner heard the Tallants, accompanied by Deputy Lucas, enter the jail.

"You all just wait a bit till I can get a light going," he heard the lawman say.

A match flared in the darkness of the office area. It was followed by a yellow glow that spread throughout the jail.

"You all want to talk to him?" Lucas asked, coming toward the cells.

"Yes, but not all at once," Martha said. "I'll go first."

A moment later the older woman, preceded by the deputy, appeared at his cell door. Producing a key, Lucas opened the barred panel. As Martha entered, Buckner got to his feet.

"Know it's a mite late for visiting," Lucas said, backing out, "but I didn't figure you'd mind."

"We're obliged to you, Deputy," Buckner said. Lucas no doubt was thinking of Henry Guzman and hoping to avoid any confrontation with him. "Time don't matter."

"About right. Make your visiting short and sweet."

Buckner put his attention on Martha. "Did you get settled all right?"

She nodded. "We did everything you said. We're comfortable at the inn, had a bath and ate supper. The horses
have all been taken care of."

"Glad to hear it. Willow's not a town for a woman to be
stranded in."

"Can see that. I want to tell you, John, how sorry we are
that things have turned out this way for you. If you hadn't
stopped to help us you'd not be in this fix."

He shrugged. "Maybe. I could've run into the detective
if I'd gone on south, or even west. Guessing what might
have happened is always easy to do."

"Perhaps. I'd better go now. I'll leave it up to Thalia to
tell you what we've decided. I just want to thank you again
and wish you good luck."

Buckner smiled, took the woman's hand into his own
and shook it gently. "Good luck to you," he said.

Martha Tallant turned and walked back into the office
area. At once Thalia, looking fresh and clean, dark hair
gathered about her face and drawn to a knot on her head,
stood before him. She smelled like lilacs after a rain
shower, and the blue dress she now wore, evidently bought
only that evening at one of the mercantiles, etched a picture on his mind that he knew he could never forget.

"Going to be hard as hell to leave you," he murmured.

In the next instant she was locked in his arms, her slim
body pressed against him while he pressed a kiss upon her
lips.

"I—I can't let you go," she said. "I just can't!"

"No choice," he said, "but I'm not saying it will be for
long. There's a lot of miles between here and Missouri and
that detective's not going to find it easy getting me there."

She drew back from him, her features filled with concern. "Do you intend to try and get away from him? Oh, John, I hope you can!" Her cheeks were wet with tears.

He glanced beyond her to where Lucas was in conversation with Martha and Augusta. "You can figure on me making a try."

"But you must be careful. He's a mean, dangerous man—"

"Know that, and it's special in his mind that he gets me back to Missouri because I took the money right out from under his nose."

Her arms went around him again. "I'll be praying for you—praying that you can escape," she said softly. "And we'll be waiting right here for you to come back."

"And I'll be back or you'll get a letter from me saying that I didn't make it—"

"You will, John, I'm sure of it," Thalia said in a confident voice, and tilting her head, kissed him again on the lips. "Remember me by that. It tells you how much I love you."

"Not much chance of me ever forgetting," Buckner said. "Just don't give up on me. Could take a while before I show up—but I will. I want you to—"

"We best be breaking this up," the deputy called. "Kind of pushing our luck as it is."

"All right," Buckner said, and taking Thalia in his arms once more, held her close and then pushed her gently toward the door.

"Deputy," he said, raising his voice slightly, "I'm asking you to look out for my women. This is a rough town and I don't want anything happening to them. Already lost one."

"Lost one?" Lucas repeated as he locked the door after Thalia. "How was that?"

"They can tell you all about it," Buckner said. He smiled at Thalia. "Tell Augusta so long for me—same to Sassy if you see her again."

"I will!" Thalia said. "She's right here in town—they were here when we got here. She and Ben are married. He sold the horses and saddles of his pa's friends to raise money. They're going on to Colorado—to some town called Denver."

"Married? With him being one of the bunch that jumped your wagon and killed your pa—how's your mama taking it?"

"He claims he took no hand in the shooting. I guess she believes him just like Sassy does. Do you?"

"He could be telling the truth. Anyway what's done is done. Your mama said something about new plans."

"Yes, we've decided to stay right here in Willow Springs. Maybe we'll start a restaurant—a home cooking place. Or we may go into the hotel business. There's no point in us going on to Colorado now."

"I guess you're right—"

"One thing more," Thalia said, lowering her voice and stepping up close to the cell as Lucas returned to his office. "I can buy a gun and slip it to you through that side window. Mama and Augusta both agreed it was a good idea."

Buckner was shaking his head even before she had finished talking. "No—I won't let—"

"It's real dark outside. Nobody'll see me."

Buckner's hands closed over hers as she grasped the iron bars that separated them. "I can't let you take that chance. Besides you can bet Guzman will search me in the morning before we move out."

"But you'll need a gun if—"

"I'll get one somehow once we're on the trail. It's best you go now. We don't want to get the deputy in trouble. Take care."

"You, too," Thalia said, and with tears glistening in her eyes and dampening her cheeks, turned and slowly rejoined her family and the deputy.

TWENTY-THREE

IT WAS COLD AND GRAY. Buckner, astride his sorrel gelding, handcuffs linking his wrists, settled into the saddle and watched Henry Guzman make a final adjustment to the packsaddle of the mule he had bought. The sun had not yet broken over the peaks of the Capulins to the east, and Willow, except for a few diehard drunks in the Animas Saloon, was still sleeping.

"Expect I'd better tell you before we head out," Guzman said, finishing with the mule's load, "if you make one wrong move you're a dead man. That clear?"

Buckner stirred indifferently. "You're holding all the high cards, Detective," he said, lifting his manacled hands in a show of captivity. "I'd be a fool to try."

Guzman nodded curtly as he swung up onto his horse. The white-stockinged black looked sleek and fit after the several days of rest and good feeding he had enjoyed. The thought rushed through Buckner's mind that if and when he got the opportunity to make a break, his sorrel, as big and strong as he was, would be no match for the detective's animal.

"You about ready?" Lucas called from the doorway of the jail.

Guzman made no reply, simply took up the lead ropes,

one to Buckner's horse, the other to the pack mule, and making use of his spurs, moved out. Buckner, raising his hands, gestured to the lawman. In that moment he straightened in the saddle. Thalia was standing near the rear of the jail watching his departure.

In the gloom she looked soft and blurred in the white dress and shawl she was wearing. When she saw that he had seen and recognized her, she lifted a hand and waved a last farewell.

A surge of unreasoning anger swept Buckner. He was getting a raw deal—just as was Thalia! Henry Guzman had no right to be taking him back to Missouri, to a prison where he'd not see freedom for years—and all because he had lost patience with the damned railroad and collected money due him in the only way they had left open to him.

"I'll be back!" he called, returning the woman's gesture. "Wait for me!"

"What's that?" Guzman demanded, twisting half about. "You talking to me?"

"No, to the lady standing there by the jail. Told her I'd be back."

Guzman laughed. "In about fifteen or twenty years, maybe."

Buckner smiled tightly. "I'll be back," he repeated, and fell into a deep silence.

The day, cloudy and cool, wore on. They were not following the route they had taken when coming from Missouri, Buckner noticed, but were bearing more to the north. It was better traveling as they were following a well-marked road which, if it continued, would get them to Grovertown in less time than the original journey west had taken.

But roads in that part of the frontier had a way of just petering out, Buckner knew, and he had little faith in it extending for any great distance. Too, if Guzman didn't eventually start bearing south, they would ride straight into No Man's Land, the outlaw stronghold in the Indian Territory panhandle. The detective would be aware of that, Buckner was certain, and held his peace until late in the morning of the second day out he noticed Guzman had not altered course.

"You know this country?" he asked. There had been practically no conversing between them since leaving Willow Springs.

"Know all I need to," the detective said gruffly.

"Maybe you don't know enough. You keep on going due east we'll end up in a nest of outlaws. You better be angling more to the south."

"I'll be deciding what we'll do!" Guzman snapped irritably. "Following this course we'll cut a day or more off traveling time to Grovertown."

"And maybe we'll never get there at all. I expect half the outlaws in the panhandle know about the five thousand dollars you've got on that mule."

Guzman pulled to a stop and swung about. "You do any talking about it?" he demanded, his features hard set and angry.

"No, but any fool would know that in a little town like Willow Springs word would get out and spread faster than a grass fire."

"You saying that fool deputy done some talking about the money?"

"No, I don't know whether he did or not," Buckner said. "News like that just has a way of getting out. You aim to turn south?"

"No, not wasting any more time than I have to—"

"Then you best give me back my gun because you're going to need all the help you can get."

Guzman laughed. "Me give you your gun? They'll be making snowballs in hell before I'd do that! I'm no looney.

The last thing I'd ever do would be to give you back your gun."

"It just could be," Buckner said quietly as they rode on.

They had broken out of the foothill country east of volcanic Capulin mountain and were moving along a dry creek. To the south and west Buckner could see the ragged formations of Sierra Grande and Laughlin peaks rising up from the flat mesa land as if hoping to pierce the overcast and reach the clear blue sky beyond.

Patches of bright yellow and deep purple flowers broke the gray-green flats and the low, red-faced buttes that were studded with white rocks. A long strip of deeper green lying well to the south marked the course of a stream or possibly a river of some size. That was where they should be doing their traveling, Buckner thought; but Henry Guzman was unrelenting in his determination to maintain a due-east course into the outlaw-infested panhandle.

They camped that night along a creek Buckner thought was called the Currampa. Guzman took no pains to conceal their presence. He built a fire for cooking a meal of already boiled potatoes, dried meat, corn, bread and coffee, and when it was over, heaped more wood on the flames to ward off the evening chill.

Buckner, recognizing the futility of protesting, said nothing other than to suggest the detective sleep with one hand on his rifle and be ready to surrender a handgun to him should it become necessary. But Guzman only shrugged off the veiled warning.

"You're just hoping it might happen so's you'll get a chance to get away," he said, stretching out on his blanket. He spent a few moments drawing the cover about his body and then pulled the small tarp that was part of his bedroll over all. "Seems to me you're real edgy for a real bad *hombre*."

"Only using good sense," Buckner said, struggling to get

comfortable in his blanket. The manacles about his wrists, and the leg irons the detective had affixed along with a short rope that anchored him to a close-by clump of juniper, made his efforts all but impossible, but he said nothing about it to Guzman; it would be like talking to the wind.

For a long time he lay motionless staring up into the murky sky. Most of the heavy clouds had drifted on without shedding any rain and now stars were slowly becoming visible. Off to the west a wolf howled into the hush. A coyote answered from somewhere to the south.

Buckner's mind shifted to Thalia, to his last look at her standing there in the half light at Willow Springs waving a good-bye. He wondered what she was doing at that early evening hour—if she were thinking of him or, possibly, having second thoughts about their future. He brushed that out of his mind. Thalia would have more faith in him than that, and while she might wonder and worry about how he could manage an escape from Henry Guzman, she'd never give up on—

Buckner's thoughts came to a full stop. The click of metal against rock registered on his hearing. He cut his eyes to the left. No doubt the sound was made by the shod hoof of a horse coming in contact with a stone.

He saw the dimly silhouetted rider in that next moment. The man had halted just beyond Guzman. He appeared to be studying the sleeping detective, and then after several moments turned and looked off to his left, and whistled softly. Apparently he wasn't alone, was now waiting for his partner, or partners, to join him.

Buckner, handicapped by the iron on his wrists, slowly worked his arms out from beneath the blanket and bit of canvas that covered him. Feeling about on the uneven ground, he located a small rock. Rising slightly, he threw it at Guzman.

The stone struck the detective on the shoulder. He rolled over at once and sat up. He saw the rider directly off to his right, no more than a dozen strides distant. He reacted instantly. His rifle bloomed, filling the night with echoes. The rider yelled, and his horse, shying suddenly, spilled the man to the ground.

"There's more of them," Buckner shouted, kicking free of his covers, and coming to his feet. "We best get the hell out of here!"

Guzman said nothing but slung his tarp and blankets across the mule. Crossing to Buckner, he cut the rope, and dug out a key to unlock the leg irons. As he turned to gather the cooking equipment, Buckner added his bed to the pack animal.

"You about ready?" he asked, looking off into the night for any signs of more outlaws.

"I am," the detective replied in a low voice as he added the sack of utensils to the mule's load. "You for damn sure he ain't alone?"

Buckner swore under his breath. "You want to wait and find out?"

The detective, a dark shape in the muted light, paused. "I ain't so sure this ain't one of your tricks. Could be doing this so's—"

"Jud?" a voice called tentatively in the night. "You spot them? Was that you shooting?"

Henry Guzman took a firm grip on the lead rope of Buckner's horse, and the pack mule.

"Move out," he said in a hoarse whisper. "We'll get over on the other side of that stand of brush. There's sort of a wash there. They won't see us leaving."

TWENTY-FOUR

THEY LED THE ANIMALS for the first few yards, hearing as they did the sounds of riders closing in on the camp. Shouts went up and they realized the outlaws had discovered the body of their member. When they were well clear of the place, they swung up into their saddles, and staying in the wash, put the horses and the reluctant mule to a slow run.

They were now following a due south course, Guzman at last taking John Buckner's suggestion. By daylight they were out of the panhandle and on Texas soil—not that such provided any safe guarantee; the area was equally wild and forsaken, and if the outlaws knew the direction their intended victims had taken, they would find a holdup as easy a task as it would have been back in No Man's Land.

Guzman said nothing about the incident, thanking Buckner neither for awakening him in time, nor for his advice to leave the lawless area so favored by renegades.

They halted around midmorning beside a small creek, built a low fire, and brewed up some coffee, using the small, blackened pot that the detective had in his grub sack. Breakfast was warmed meat and biscuits washed down by the strong, thick drink.

"Looks like we shook that bunch," the detective said as they were finishing off the last of the coffee.

"We had some luck that time," Buckner agreed.

"You figure they'll be trailing us?"

Buckner's expression changed to surprise. For Henry Guzman to ask his opinion on anything was a radical change.

"Doubt it," he said.

The detective took a final swallow of the coffee and glanced to the sky. It had cleared and now was a bright, brilliant blue stretching from horizon to horizon.

"Sure surprised you didn't try to make a run for it," he said.

Buckner shrugged. "I'll pick a time when my chances will be better."

"They won't get no better'n that," Guzman said, getting to his feet, and starting to collect gear. "That was as good as you'll ever see. Let's move out."

They struck due east across the grassy flats, stopping early for night in the lea of a red earth butte that was not far from water. Conversation between them was again as it had been in the beginning—almost nonexistent. The grim silence did not bother Buckner; he was a man accustomed to his own company, a trait acquired, no doubt, during the years he had drifted about the frontier by himself.

Too, talking with Henry Guzman was far from a pleasure. The detective was a morose, opinionated, single-minded man who had but one thought in mind and that was to return to Grovertown with his prisoner as soon as possible, and in so doing, Buckner suspected, prove his worth to the railroad.

They encountered no more outlaws and on the fifth day left Texas and were again in Indian Territory. It was high plains country, all grassy flats, red hills and soil of similar color. There were no trees of size but a wealth of bayonet yucca, cactus, snakeweed and the like. It was all new to Guzman but fairly familiar to John Buckner as it was not greatly unlike the rest of the frontier southwest and west over which he had wandered.

Guzman appeared to have gotten his bearings. They were angling across the Indian Territory for its upper northeast corner where they would enter Missouri. It was the most direct route and considerable time would be saved in doing so. The only drawback was the danger from renegade Indians who refused to adhere to the Treaties and persisted in their attacks on pilgrims who crossed what they considered their land. Some were Cheyennes, remnants of the war party led by a chief called Stone Calf, who had become partner with the Kiowas a year or so earlier when they made a concerted effort to drive all whites off the plains country.

Buckner had encountered a small hunting party whose attitudes toward the whites were unknown, earlier as he made his way west with Guzman and the posse on his trail. He hoped the detective and he would have better luck and not run into any of the braves, although such just might provide the opportunity for escape that he was continually looking for.

But that had another side to it. They were still several days from the Missouri border, and it was best he be more practical in his thinking. They could both lose their scalps in an all out fight with a band of vengeful warriors.

"Do you know right where we are?" he asked, shifting his weight in the saddle. The wound in his leg had begun to trouble him in the past day or two, and he was continually forced to favor it.

"Expect I do," Guzman replied, irritated as always by Buckner's questioning his decisions. "Can't be more than a couple of days to the border."

"More like three, maybe four. All depends."

"Depends on what?" the detective demanded. "Weather's good. Only rain we've spotted is back there in those mountains in New Mexico."

"Not talking about rain, talking about renegade Indians. Plenty of them on the prowl through here."

"Hell! There ain't been no sign of any."

"That's no proof they're not around. We'd be smart to swing south for a spell, do our traveling along that band of brush and scrub oaks."

Guzman followed the line of Buckner's pointing finger. "That'd cost us a half day, maybe more."

"Could cost you your life—mine, too. Lot of braves still on the warpath along here."

"I was told they'd all settled down and were peaceable."

"Most have but there's still raiding going on—small war parties jumping pilgrims passing through, or burning isolated farms and ranches in Kansas and Texas, and other places. My advice is for us to get over to that line of brush I showed you. It probably runs along a big wash or arroyo where we can take cover if we have to."

Henry Guzman turned his head and spat in disgust. "You don't know that—you're just talking. Like I said we ain't seen any hostiles—not since we left that town. Could be that brush is where you're aiming to try an escape."

"Wasn't thinking of it, but now I am," Buckner replied coolly. "What's bothering me right now is that we're out in the open. Can be seen for miles."

Guzman made no comment. They continued on following the same course, moving directly across the empty flats for the northeastern corner of the Territory.

They were traveling at a fairly good pace. The very contour of the land had favored them, being flat and firm, but now they were entering a spread of low hills. Too, the band of brush was now curving north, toward them. They would soon be able to take advantage of it despite Guzman's hard-headed attitude.

Buckner, resting his weight on his good leg, raised himself in the stirrup and swept the surrounding country with probing eyes. An uneasiness filled him. He could feel it in his bones—in the air.

In that next moment shrill yells broke out. A rifle shot shattered the hush. Dust spurted up from the ground a short distance behind them. Looking back hurriedly, Buckner saw a half dozen or so braves racing toward them from a hollow in the low hills.

"Head for the brush!" he yelled to Guzman, and veered the sorrel hard right, thankful that days earlier the detective had decided the lead rope he'd tied to the sorrel was no longer necessary and removed it.

Bent low over the big red horse's neck, he flung a glance at Guzman. The detective had put his horse into a dead run for the strip of brush, and was firing his revolver at the yelling braves. He had dropped the mule's rope in order to use both hands. The pack animal, accustomed to being with the horses, was galloping along in close pursuit despite the lack of a tether.

The Indians, unencumbered by saddles and other gear, gained steadily. The one with a rifle was drawing within range, his bullets now kicking up dust and debris dangerously close. Buckner, cursing his lack of a weapon with which to fight back, looked ahead. The brush and possible safety were still some distance away. At once he veered the sorrel toward Guzman.

"Throw me your rifle!"

The detective, ruddy, bewhiskered features grim, shook his head. "Keep riding! We'll be all right when we get to that brush!"

If we get to the brush, Buckner thought, and flattened out more on the sorrel. The yells of the braves, Kiowas, he thought—or they could be Comanches—echoed about him. The one with the rifle, marksmanship leaving something to be desired, was drawing nearer to Guzman.

One of the braves faltered on his horse and began to pull away. Guzman had managed to hit one of them but it went unnoticed by the others, who continued to close in. They were near enough to see the sweaty, glistening copper of their skin, their black hair held in place by a narrow strip of cloth. As they hunched low on their ponies, narrow faces thrust forward, teeth bared, eerie screeches and unnerving howls continued to issue from their throats.

That there was only one with a rifle was certain. Buckner saw three of the remaining with bows and arrows while the rest had lances. The odds were down a little, he thought. Guzman had accounted for one of the party but there were still six to be reckoned with, all, thankfully, armed only with primitive weapons.

Small puffs of smoke from Guzman's weapon and the brave's rifle began to hang in the motionless air. The wild yells of the Indians, sensing a victory, grew louder.

"Give me a gun!" Buckner shouted again to the detective as he slowed and veered in close. "We're not going to make it!"

The detective, at last facing reality, leaned forward and drew the weapon from the boot. Surging in toward the sorrel, he tossed the gun to Buckner.

John immediately jacked a cartridge into the chamber, and sighting as best he could down the barrel, pressed off a shot at the nearest brave. The Indian threw up his hands, slid from the back of his spotted pony, and fell to the ground, his body bouncing limply upon impact.

The yells of the remaining braves grew louder. Buckner risked a glance at the line of brush. It was not too far now. He turned to look at Henry Guzman. The Indians, having noticed that only Guzman was firing at them and guessing the other rider was unarmed, had been concentrating their attack on the detective. Their tactics now changed. Three of the braves veered away from their pursuit of Guzman, and focussed their attention on Buckner.

Arrows began to sail past him, making their peculiar hissing sound. Spurring the sorrel for more speed, he snapped a shot at one of the three closing in on him, saw the man wilt and fall from his horse. He became aware then that the detective was no longer firing his weapon, and turned to look. Guzman was slumped in his saddle. An arrow was sticking stiffly out of his back. A second brave was racing in, bow drawn, arrow aimed. Guzman twisted about and triggered a bullet in the direction of the brave. The bullet missed.

Suddenly he stiffened as the brave with the rifle followed up with a shot. Guzman sagged, clawed at his horse's mane to keep from falling. Buckner, firing steadily through the dust and confusion of yelling, slowed. Taking better aim, he leveled on the brave with the rifle and squeezed the trigger. The Indian, his mouth blared open as he voiced a yell, suddenly stiffened and fell. Cool, Buckner sighted in on another of the bucks, seeing from the corner of his eye as he did the mule slow, stagger and go down in an explosion of dust and litter.

John pressed off another shot, saw the brave he'd targeted rock to one side and fall. John cast a glance over his shoulder. The brush was only yards away. He swerved in close to Guzman.

"Hang on! We've almost made it!"

The detective stirred weakly. He was having difficulty staying on his horse and unable to do anything to protect himself.

Curving away from the detective, Buckner sighted as best he could on the nearest brave. The bullet drove into the man's chest. The yell he was voicing froze on his lips, and as his horse slowed, he tumbled to the ground.

At once the remaining braves, abruptly silent, began to swing off. Buckner, sliding the rifle in his saddle boot, veered to Guzman. Seizing the trailing reins of the black, and unsure of the remaining braves and of the possibility of there being a larger party nearby, he hurriedly rode into the brush. A good-sized wash lay beyond, and he continued on east into it. The Indians, if they returned, would know where he had entered the band of cover and would expect him and his wounded partner to be there, or close by. He would not make it that easy for them; he'd ride on for a mile or so and then pull well off to the side. He had to see what he could do for Henry Guzman.

TWENTY-FIVE

BUCKNER DREW TO A HALT in a grove of pin oaks a quarter mile off the trail. After dismounting quickly he turned to Guzman. He gently pulled him from the saddle, and laid him on his side in the thick accumulation of leaves.

"Damn it all—I expect I'm done for," the detective muttered. "Hit pretty bad."

"I'll see what I can do," Buckner replied, examining the arrow. Taking it in his hands, he tested it carefully. The point was in deep and firmly embedded. "That one's not going to come out easy."

"What I figured. Break it off close to the skin. Maybe it won't bother me so much then. What about the bullet?"

"In deep, too," Buckner said. "Need to get you to a doctor."

"Ain't likely to be one around anywheres close," Guzman said irritably. "How far are we from home?"

"Five days—could be six. Hold on, I'll break off that arrow like you want."

Taking Guzman's knife from its sheath, and as gentle as possible, Buckner cut a groove in the arrow near the point where it had entered the detective's body. That done, he took the shaft in both hands and snapped it. Guzman groaned and swore deeply.

"It done?"

Buckner held up the two pieces of the feathered wood. "Done. Next thing we better do is stop the bleeding."

Guzman shook his head. With most of the arrow's length removed he was able to partly lay on his back.

"Got medicine and such in the pack on the mule. Them damned Indians went and shot it down—"

"You stay quiet. I'm going after the pack," Buckner said, getting to his feet.

"You sure that's what you'll be doing?" the detective asked, a half sneer wiping the pain from his face. "You been looking for the chance to get away from me—looks like it's come."

Buckner favored the detective with a pitying look. Only a man like Guzman would think of such a cold-blooded, heartless thing. But there was some value in the idea. He owed Henry Guzman nothing—and the chances the detective would survive his wounds were very small.

"Your gun's in my saddlebags—so's the money. You might as well have them both."

At Guzman's words Buckner turned, crossed to where the detective's horse was standing. Opening the right hand pocket, he took out his belt and gun and strapped them on. The money he found under a bit of clothing in the opposite pocket, and he stowed it away in his own leather bags.

Guzman eyes this sourly as he mounted the sorrel. "You aim to come back now?"

"I'll be back," Buckner replied, and rode off.

Now that the detective had put the idea of escape in his mind John Buckner gave it thought. He'd need only to take some of the trail grub from the pack on the dead mule and head west. Thalia would be waiting for him at Willow Springs, and while he'd have to avoid Deputy Lucas, they could slip away and either head south for Arizona or north into Colorado.

Buckner swore softly. What the hell was the matter with him? He was thinking like Guzman, putting himself down in the same class. As much as he'd like to join Thalia Tallant, be with her for the rest of their lives, he couldn't pay that kind of cost. He'd never be at peace with himself again.

Retracing his trail through the brush and arroyo, Buckner reached the point where he had entered. Halting there, he looked out onto the hilly plain. Scouring the area carefully for any sign of the Indians, and seeing none, Buckner rode quickly to where the mule lay. Guzman's knife in hand, he dismounted, and hunching beside the mule, already drawing hordes of flies, cut the pack-saddle cinches. Throwing it up behind the cantle of the hull on the sorrel, he remounted and returned hurriedly to where he had left Henry Guzman.

The detective greeted him with disbelief in his eyes. "Didn't expect you to come back."

"Said I would, didn't I?" Buckner snapped, a little weary of the detective's mistrust. He removed the pack saddle from the sorrel. "You hurting bad?"

"Plenty," Guzman muttered.

Buckner said nothing as he dug into one of the sacks for a pan in which to heat water. Finding a lard tin, he poured a small quantity into it from one of the canteens and turned to build a fire. Evidently there had been less rain in the area than farther west and he found dry wood easily available. While the water was heating, he searched the other sacks, found a strip of white cloth which he tore into bandages. The water was hot by then, and folding one of the strips into a pad, he removed Guzman's blood-soaked shirt and cleaned both wounds.

He was fooling no one, he realized as he applied the disinfectant he'd taken from the sack. Guzman's wounds would mortify soon unless they were taken care of properly. Making two pads from the bit of cotton cloth, he soaked both with disinfectant, placed them over the wounds, and bound them in place with bandages. He was unable to wrap the wound properly because of the shortened shaft sticking out as it did, but he did manage to slow the bleeding to some extent.

"You hungry?" he asked when he was finished and was stowing the medicine and leftover cloth in the sack.

Guzman shook his head. "Not much. Could use a drink but I guess coffee'll have to do. That water still hot?"

"Sure is. I'll stir up a couple of cups, then we better ride, get out of this country." Crossing to the detective's horse, he took a clean shirt from the saddlebags, helped the man put it on along with his vest. "Too many hostiles around here to suit me."

They were mounted and on their way within a half hour. It was painful for Henry Guzman, Buckner knew, but there was no help for it, and the man bore up well, sometimes riding slumped forward in the saddle, other times hanging sideways as if he were about to fall from his horse.

Three days later, after they had made camp Buckner could see that the detective was failing steadily. He had weakened despite all that he'd been able to do for the man, and it was apparent he was soon done for unless proper medical aid was provided. Accordingly the next morning Buckner swung inward from the trail, and around midmorning spotted a farmhouse back in a clearing. As he rode into the yard a man in bib overalls and straw hat, with a double-barreled shotgun hung in the crook of an elbow, came out onto the narrow porch that fronted the sod and wood structure.

"Ran into some hostiles back aways," Buckner said, getting to the point immediately. "My partner stopped a bullet and's got an arrow in him. There a doctor anywhere close?"

"Not for maybe a couple of days' ride," the man said in a nasal voice. "My woman's sort of a nurse. Maybe she can help."

"Expect she can—leastwise she can do more for him than I can. Where'll I take him?" Buckner said, dismounting, and reaching up for Guzman.

"You willing to pay?" the farmer asked.

"I'll pay," Buckner answered impatiently. "The man's in a bad way. Where do I take him—he's too weak to walk. I'll have to carry him."

"Bring him through here," a woman's voice directed from the doorway.

Buckner gave her a quick, grateful glance, took Guzman in his arms, and carried him up onto the porch and into the house.

"There's a bed in that room off to the right. Put him in there."

Buckner laid the barely conscious Guzman on the arrangement of mat-covered boards and small barrels that once contained horseshoe nails, and stepped back. The woman, bending over the detective, removed the bandages and pads. She examined the wounds and shook her head.

"Mighty bad. That arrow and that bullet have got to come out. He's got a lot of fever—how long have they been in him?"

"Four days more or less. Did what I could for him but I—"

"Well, I ain't no doctor, and I ain't had a lot of practice taking arrows and bullets out of a body, but if you like, I'll try."

"No choice—go ahead," Buckner said.

"Now, you won't be blaming her none if he croaks, will you?" the husband asked, his eyes on the deputy sheriff star pinned to Guzman's vest.

"No—"

"He a lawman?"

Buckner nodded. "A detective. What's your name?"

"Shoemaker. Mattie there is my wife. I'm Caleb."

"Friends call me John," Buckner said, not liking the interest Shoemaker was taking in Guzman being a lawman.

"Can't you get busy on my partner?" he said, turning to the woman. "He's hurting bad."

"Sure can, but you menfolk will have to help me," Mattie replied. "Get that vest and shirt off him while I go fetch some hot water. And I'll be needing that bottle of chloroform that army doctor left me, Caleb. Get it."

The farmer nodded, and together they both walked back into the rear of the house. Buckner quickly removed Guzman's clothing. The detective was ghost white and burning hot with fever, but he knew Guzman for a strong man, and now the proper things were to be done, he felt the chances for his recovery were better.

"Turn him over on his belly," Mattie directed as she returned to the room.

"Who's that?" Guzman muttered feebly.

"A nurse. She's going to fix you up," John answered as he followed the woman's instructions.

Guzman mumbled something unintelligible. Caleb came in with the anesthetic. Mattie poured a small quantity on a pad and held it to Guzman's nose and mouth. When the man was totally relaxed she climbed up on the bed, and straddling the detective, motioned to the two men.

"He's out cold, but I reckon one of you better hold down his legs, the other one his shoulders. Just might come to at the wrong time."

Buckner and Caleb took their places, and the woman, having dipped a slim-bladed knife and a pair of tweezers into the scalding water, began to work on the embedded arrow. Guzman groaned, endeavored to pull away.

Mattie paused. "Sure in there deep," she said. "Now,

keep him from moving. Can't do nothing with him squirming about."

The woman went back to her surgery, removing the arrow after considerable effort, and then the bullet which proved to be much less trouble. That accomplished, she cleaned both wounds with disinfectant of some kind, applied a greenish-looking ointment of her own concoction, according to Caleb, and finished off by placing pads and a bandage over the wounds much as Buckner had done earlier.

"Best you let him lay there for a spell," Mattie said. "Till morning at least. Then you get him to a regular doctor. Them wounds could mortify."

"You think he'll make it?" Buckner asked.

"Expect he will—he's a strong one. We can put you up for the night if you want."

"You'll have to pay—" Caleb said.

"I intend to. You can tell me how much in the morning. Right now I'd like to take care of the horses."

"The barn's out back," Shoemaker said. "Mind, don't go wasting any of that grain. Costs money."

"I'll pay for it, too," Buckner said, and with a glance at the unconscious Henry Guzman, returned to the yard and led the horses to the barn. As he led the animals into the shelter it suddenly occurred to him that the detective in no way would be able to sit his saddle for the long haul ahead. Throwing some grain in the mangers of the two stalls in which the horses were now standing, he forked down a little hay, and returned to the house. Caleb was sitting in his rocking chair in the front room smoking a charred briar pipe.

"Need to make a drag for my partner," Buckner said, looking about the room. The walls had been whitewashed and several framed pictures of relatives and probably friends, along with two or three feed company calendar prints, graced the smooth surfaces. "Have you got a couple of long poles I can use? They'll have to be—"

"I reckon I know how to make a drag," Shoemaker cut in dryly. "Sure, I can fix you up. You'll be needing some canvas, too, and some straps or ropes."

"Whatever you've got," Buckner said. "Aim to get it together today. Be pulling out early in the morning."

Caleb removed the pipe from his mouth. "Which horse will you be using?"

"The black one—"

Shoemaker stuffed the pipe into his shirt pocket. "I reckon we best get started at it. Can find most of what you're needing in the barn." Rising, the farmer started for the door. He paused, looked back. "You that deputy's prisoner?"

John Buckner had been expecting the question ever since Shoemaker had noted Guzman's badge. He grinned, shrugged. "You think I'd be fool enough to be looking after him if I was?"

The farmer rubbed at his jaw. "No, I reckon not," he said, and headed for the barn.

TWENTY-SIX

JOHN BUCKNER halted at the edge of Grovertown and considered what lay ahead for him. It was late morning and only a few townspeople were abroad. Dusty, bearded, eyes red-rimmed from lack of sleep, and bone tired, he searched his memory for the location of the doctor's office. If he could reach it without drawing attention, and turn Guzman over to the physician, he might be able to slip back out of town and be on his way to Willow Springs and Thalia without further trouble.

The doctor's office was at the far end of the street, he recalled—or at least that's where it was when he was familiar with the settlement. A groan from Henry Guzman on his belly on the drag drew his attention. It had been a long, hard trip, one during which he had halted several times, as instructed by Mattie Shoemaker, to change the dressing of the wounds and apply a fresh coating of disinfectant from the jar the slightly built, graying woman gave him. Guzman's fever had abated after Mattie had removed the bullet and Kiowa arrow from his body, and had remained down, much to Buckner's relief. He knew he could do little if anything about it should it return, other than increase their pace and travel well into the night.

He realized it was the same as opening the cell door once

he started down the street and was seen. And after that, thanks to the influence of the railroad, would come years in the penitentiary. He was fully aware of all that but John Buckner, adhering to the only code he could live by, had no other answer.

Still Henry Guzman might die from his wounds, and all the hardship involved in getting him to Grovertown, and sacrificing his own freedom could be for nothing. But it was not in Buckner to look at it in that light; the detective, a tough old rooster as someone had described him, was alive and probably would remain so.

Shrugging, Buckner raked his horse with spurs, and tightening his grip on the black's lead rope, started down the street. Off to the right in the homes that lay scattered about on the grassy, meadow-like flat a dog began to bark, and over at the Christian Church on the far side of town the bell began to toll, mournfully lamenting the death of some local citizen.

Faces began to appear in the windows of the weather-beaten stores and residences along the way. When he drew abreast the bank C. W. Pruitt appeared suddenly in the doorway. A little farther on two men, both vaguely familiar, drew together hastily and started to converse. Before Buckner had gone a dozen yards they wheeled and half ran toward the sheriff's office and jail. A hard grin tugged at the corners of John Buckner's mouth; now it would all start.

It didn't matter. He knew it was coming and was ready for it. He'd give the law no trouble, just go ahead and take what was coming to him. The only thing Buckner didn't feel in his heart was that he'd done anything wrong.

A long sigh escaped his lips. On his left, and not on ahead as he'd expected to find the doctor, he saw the sign: HORATIO JONES M.D. Immediately he veered the sorrel toward it, and the black, poles of the drag grating on the sandy soil, followed wearily.

Jones, a middle-aged man in white shirt, with sleeves rolled up to the elbows, dark pants and vest, spectacles raised and clinging to his forehead, appeared at once on the porch of the clapboard house. He hurried to Buckner.

"What is it? Who—" he began, and peered closer at the man on the drag. He straightened up. "Why, it's Henry Guzman!"

A murmur ran through the crowd that had gathered quickly. Buckner stepped down from the sorrel. "He's been shot in the back. Took an arrow there, too. I got him doctored up as best I could."

"He's about dead," Jones said. "Get him inside." He beckoned to the crowd. "Some of you men carry him into my office." Still all business, the physician turned to Buckner. "You don't look much better than he does. Anything wrong with you?"

Buckner shook his head. "Can use some sleep—"

"Then go get it," Jones said, and followed the quartet of men who had lifted Guzman from the drag and were taking him into the physician's office.

Buckner came about, drew up stiffly. A man wearing a deputy's badge, flanked by Pruitt and the two men he'd seen conversing, faced him. The lawman, elderly with a snow-white handlebar mustache and pointed beard, had his right hand resting on the butt of the pistol hanging at his side.

"If you're John Buckner you're under arrest," he said. "Don't give me any trouble."

Buckner's shoulders stirred slightly. He was too spent to put up any opposition even if he were of a mind to.

"No trouble, Deputy," he said to the lawman, a stranger to him. He glanced at Pruitt. "The money's in my saddle-bags."

"What happened?" one of the men with the banker asked. "Where's Simmons and Trevitt? We figured they'd be with you."

"Never saw them," Buckner replied. "They pulled out a few days ahead of Guzman and me."

"How'd Henry get shot?"

"A bunch of Indians jumped us over the Territory."

"How come you brought him in?" someone wondered. "You was his prisoner—"

"Didn't have no choice," Buckner said. "Couldn't go off and leave him there," he added as the deputy snapped handcuffs about his wrists. "I'll take it as a favor if one of you will see to the horses."

"I'll take care of them," the lawman said, and taking Buckner's gun from its holster, grasped him by the arm and moved off for the jail.

"Judge'll be coming to town—Judge Carpenter—in three or four days," the deputy said as he locked John in one of the jail's four cells. "Like as not he'll hold your trial first off. Feeling's going to be running kind of strong against you."

"Why? All I did was collect my own money from the bank."

"Just about everybody figures that was plain robbery, and around here the bank and the railroad are top dogs. And once it gets out that Simmons and Trevitt ain't back, too, there'll be them that'll figure you killed them."

"They'll be plenty wrong. Can talk to Guzman for proof of that."

"They can if he lives. There anything you want?"

"Can use something to eat—and a drink if it's not against the law. Ought to clean up a bit, too."

The deputy nodded. "I'll do what I can. I'm new here so I don't know how far I can go," and giving the cell door an extra jerk to test the lock, turned and left the building.

* * *

The courtroom was an empty building just south of Horn's General Store. It was also used occasionally for town meetings and such social affairs as dancing and tableaus put on by the Women's Aid Society of the church.

Rested, shaved and wearing a change of clothing, Buckner was led in—handcuffed once more—by the deputy and deposited in the chair reserved for the accused. There was no jury, the judge assuming full responsibility for determining guilt or innocence and passing sentence, if necessary after hearing the crime detailed by a prosecutor and a defense presented by a lawyer or the accused himself.

"Daniel Tripp's going to do the prosecuting, you still saying you don't need a lawyer?" the deputy, whose name turned out to be Tom Pierce, asked, looking out over the crowded room.

"No need," Buckner said. "Never have denied what I did. Just saying it was my own money."

"Yeh, reckon that's how it was," Pierce said, and moving around behind John, sat down.

Few of the faces in the well-filled room were familiar. Buckner did recognize some, mostly men he'd known before he'd gone off to war or else were members of the posse.

"Here's the judge," Pierce announced, and added, "Everybody stand up."

There was a noisy scraping of chair legs against the bare floor along with rustling of clothing as the jurist came into the room through a rear door of the building and made his way to a chair and table that were to serve as the bench.

Buckner closely studied the man who was to pass judgment on him. Eli Carpenter was a short, lean man with florid face, reddish hair neatly parted in the center. He had a salt and pepper beard, no mustache and small, hard eyes of indeterminate color. He was, of course, a stranger to

Buckner, and the thought passed through his mind that he could expect little compassion from the man.

"Sit down," Carpenter said with a wave of his hand. "Before we get started somebody prop open the doors. It's a little warm in here . . . Is everybody ready?"

A tall, young man with a narrow face and dressed in a somewhat rumpled gray suit, complete with bow tie, arose.

"That's Tripp," the deputy whispered. "He's a real humdinger when it comes to prosecuting."

Buckner only shrugged and stared out through the now open doorway onto the street. A man and a woman, late for the proceedings, had pulled up to the hitchrack fronting the building and were hurriedly climbing from their buggy.

"Yes, sir, Your Honor, we're all here except for the railroad detective. He's still under the doctor's care."

"Seems to me the most important witness in the case is missing," the judge said impatiently. "It would have been better to postpone the hearing until he could attend—but let's go ahead. How does the prisoner plead?"

"If it please Your Honor," Tripp said, "we have a witness equally as important as Detective Guzman who will—"

"How does the prisoner plead?" Carpenter broke in, impatience again sharpening his tone.

Buckner felt all eyes in the courtroom on him as he got to his feet. In the hush a large bluebottle fly buzzed noisily against one of the dusty windowpanes.

"If you're asking if I'm guilty of taking money from the bank that was owed me by the railroad, then I expect I am."

A murmur ran through the courtroom. Carpenter banged on the table with the small mallet he carried with him in lieu of a gavel.

"All right, if you're pleading guilty to the charge I don't see much point in holding a trial. All that's left to do is sentence you. However, you've got a right to speak out. Have you got anything to say in your own defense?"

Buckner could see no advantage in going over something that he was convinced the judge had already heard, but he was being given an opportunity to tell his side of it, and for Thalia's sake, as well as his own, he should take advantage of it.

"The railroad went ahead and bought my property while I was away fighting the war. I didn't have anything to say about it until it was all done."

A murmur again ran through the onlookers, many of whom no doubt had a similar experience with the railroad.

"They agreed to pay me five thousand dollars for my farm. I waited around five years for the money. Never did come, so one day I went and collected."

"Is that the way you understand it, Mr. Tripp?" the judge asked.

"Well, yes, Your Honor. But the point is he actually robbed the bank with a gun in his hand. The railroad's detective was present along with Mr. Pruitt, the banker, and his clerk, who unfortunately is missing."

"That true?" Carpenter asked, leaning forward.

"Yes, I reckon it is."

Carpenter settled back, a frown on his face as he fingered his beard. Tripp motioned to a well-dressed man sitting nearby, and brought him to his feet.

"Your Honor, this gentleman is Mr. Sullivan. He represents the railroad. He's here to see that justice is done in this matter, and that you assess this outlaw the full penalty the law allows for the crime he has committed. There has been far too many such robberies—"

"I know what's going on in this country, Counselor," Carpenter broke in, his face darkening. "You don't need to tell me. And as far as assessing penalty, that, I remind you, is my province."

"Yes, sir, Your Honor," Tripp said, and sat down.

Eli Carpenter fixed his cold gaze on Buckner. Anger showed in his stern features. "I think you are an honest man, John Buckner, and the railroad was not only at fault in not living up to its agreement, but in making you an outlaw."

Tripp started to rise, settled back down as the judge shook his head warningly.

"However, you were wrong to go about collecting the money the way you did. Any way you look at it, it was a holdup at gunpoint. Don't you agree?"

Buckner shrugged. "Judge, it was my money. They owed it to me. I just got tired of waiting and went in and got it. With the detective sitting right there I had to show my gun."

"And then you locked all three men in a closet—"

"Yes, sir. Needed time to get to my horse and ride out."

Carpenter looked off to one side and rubbed at his jaw. "I understand, but—"

His words halted as a commotion broke out near the rear door of the hall. Horatio Jones, a paper in his hand, bustled into the room. Hurrying, the physician laid the sheet before the judge.

"What's this?" Carpenter asked, frowning.

"Henry—Henry Guzman's in no condition to be here, Eli—I mean Your Honor. But he said he wanted to have his say."

"So he said it to you—"

"No, actually dictated it. My wife witnessed him signing the paper after I wrote it down."

Carpenter pursed his lips and studied the paper. "It says here," he began, and paused as Tripp came to his feet.

"Your Honor, this is highly irregular—"

"Could be," Carpenter replied, motioning the lawyer to silence. ". . . that he, Guzman, owes his life to the prisoner. That while he takes no stock in what the man did, he wouldn't be alive now if Buckner hadn't stayed and helped him after he was shot when he could have taken the money and made an escape. The detective feels that this should all be taken into consideration before I pass sentence."

"Your Honor—it's not relevant—" Tripp shouted, on his feet again.

Carpenter froze the man with a cold look, and placing his fingertips together, leaned back in his chair. He seemed oblivious to the murmuring in the courtroom.

"But Your Honor!" Tripp protested, half rising. "I don't think any of that should have a bearing on the sentence that should be imposed on this outlaw. He—"

"Sit back down, Mr. Prosecutor—it happens I do," the judge said, and turned to the still-standing Buckner. "I've got no choice under the law but to find you guilty of staging a bank robbery and sentencing you to twenty years in the state penitentiary."

Buckner drew up stiffly. Twenty years! He could forget all about Thalia and a future with her on some small ranch or farm.

"But I am hereby suspending the sentence and dropping all charges against you. And—"

Tripp was up once more. "Your Honor, I never heard—"

"Well, you've heard of it now, Counselor," Carpenter said coldly, "and if you jump up out of the chair one more time you're going to jump yourself into ten days in jail for contempt!"

"Yes, sir, Your Honor," Tripp said contritely.

Buckner felt as if a clean, cold wind right off a mountaintop had suddenly brushed his face, giving him life, giving him hope.

"Furthermore, I am directing the bank to hand over the

money due you today—as soon as you leave this room. Court adjourned.''

Ignoring Tripp's protests, Carpenter banged on the table with his makeshift gavel, and turned, left through the rear door. A few cheers had gone up at the judge's final words. Banker Pruitt, having a hurried conversation with the railroad's representative and Tripp, pushed his way through the exiting crowd to Buckner's side.

"The money's over at my place. I can send for it or you can drop by and pick it up."

Buckner, in a daze from the quick change in the situation, nodded. He felt the handcuffs being removed from his wrists.

"I'll be by soon as I get my horse and gear." His words had a lift to them. He was free—and he was going back to Willow Springs where Thalia was waiting for him.

"You leaving town right away?" Pierce asked. "Was hoping you'd lead me and a posse to where you think them Indians could've grabbed Simmons and that other fellow."

Relief was now flowing through John Buckner, replacing the despair and tension that had gripped him. All the hopes and dreams he'd entertained for himself and Thalia Tallant were once more alive in his mind.

"I'd like to, Deputy, but I'm going to be in a hurry."

"I see—"

"I guess you and your posse could ride with me when I leave. When we get to where the Indians jumped the detective and me I'll show you. I'll keep going but you could start looking."

"That'll sure be of a big help. Hated going out stone cold."

"Like to ask a favor of you now," Buckner said, heading for the door of the now empty room. "I'd appreciate it if you'd tell Henry Guzman I'm obliged to him—and good luck."

"Be no trouble at all. You want to move out soon?"

"Just as soon as I collect my money from the bank and get my horse," Buckner replied, and hurried on.

The Man Behind the Book

*"I appreciate my readers' loyalty. I've tried to never let them down with
a second-rate story—and I won't."*

No Western author has been more faithful to his fans than
Robert Raymond Hogan, a man known as Mr. Western by Old
West fans in over 100 countries around the world. Since the
appearance of *Ex-Marshal* (1956), his first Western novel, Ray
Hogan has produced entertaining Western stories of consistent
quality and historical significance at a breakneck pace.

This prolific author's credentials rank him among the great
Western writers of all time. Hogan's credits include 145 novels,
and over 225 articles and short stories. His works have been
filmed, televised, and translated into nineteen foreign languages.

*"I'm a person with a great love for the American West, and respect
for the people who developed it. I don't think we give enough credit to
the pioneers who moved west of the Missouri in the early days."*

Ray Hogan's ancestors first arrived in America from Northern
Ireland in 1810. Commencing with his great-grandfather who
journeyed from Pennsylvania to Kansas around 1825, losing his
life to Osage or Pawnee Indians, the Hogan family history is one
of western migration. His grandfather moved from Tennessee to
Missouri, and his father began a law enforcement career as an
early Western marshal in the Show-Me State before moving to
New Mexico when Ray was five years old.

The wild frontier of yesterday is simply family to Ray Hogan.
His lawman father met and talked with Frank James after the
famous outlaw was released from jail, and once suffered a serious
stab wound in the chest while bringing a train robber to justice.
Ray's wife, Lois Easterday Clayton, is the daughter of a New

Mexico family with its own pioneer heritage. Her grandfather began commuting between New Mexico and Missouri by horseback and stage in 1872 as a circuit-riding Methodist preacher "with a rifle across his knees." At one time he encountered the Dalton gang in Missouri.

Ray Hogan's boyhood was spent hunting, fishing, and riding horses in the New Mexico backcountry; observing all that was said and done on working ranches; and cocking an ear in hotel lobbies while railroad men, rodeo performers, townsmen, and cowhands talked about life on the range. It was only natural he decided to devote his lifetime to firsthand examination of the Old West.

Ray Hogan is a meticulous researcher, his investigations having taken him all over the West. An extensive personal library of books, pamphlets, maps, pictures, and miscellaneous data attest to his ravenous appetite for Western details. Throughout his intense, lifelong study he has painstakingly strived for authenticity.

Readers equate a Ray Hogan Western with excellence. His trademark is a good story full of human interest and action set against a factual Western background.

"I've attempted to capture the courage and bravery of those men and women that lived out West, and the dangers and problems they had to overcome."

Ray Hogan still resides in The Land of Enchantment with his equally talented wife, Lois, an accomplished artist and designer. This outstanding American continues to deliver in a way unsurpassed by his peers, keeping the Old West alive for those of us who missed it.